H.M. Patel is an avid consumer of storytelling and world-creating formats, he reads and writes fictional short stories and holds regular tabletop roleplaying games. From a young age, Computer games and movies captivated his attention, inspiring him to study Video game design and Animation at Teesside University, where he developed a keen sense of story structure and character development.

Noticing the similarities between real-life experiences and his heroes in fictional stories, he embarked on the journey of self-publishing. With the aid of friends and family, H.M. Patel writes short crime novellas for Amazon KDP, hoping to one day become a full-time author.

Sebastian Moretti & The Beasts of Shadow

H.M. Patel

Fort Gamboge

Louise

Venture Beyond

Hayden McTavish

A gem amongst pebbles

In fields of pebbles, where rocks are few,
A gemstone hides, its beauty true.
Amongst the plain, the ordinary grey,
It glimmers bright, in its own way.

The pebbles, dull and rough, they lie,
The gemstone, smooth and shining high.
It sparkles like a jewel in the sun,
A treasure found, before the day is done.

In fields of pebbles, where rocks are few,
A gemstone hides, its beauty true.
So search and find, with heart so pure,
And bring the gemstone to life, for sure.

Cold mornings were few and far between at Fort Gamboge, the sun had not yet fully risen and the air was cool with dew, speckles of moisture danced in the air which blurred the distant foliage, shapes of green and brown moulded the landscape. In the early hours of the morning the streets surrounding the Fort were barren, the hustle of the office workers rushing their kids to school to get to work before that 9 am deadline hadn't yet begun. The soft breeze rustled the trees, a distinct white noise that was the calm before the storm. The smell of menthol cigarettes filled the front security gatehouse, A small makeshift hut that housed two officers and a kitchenette, built over thirty years ago, the place could do with a serious spruce up, damp spots gathered in each corner of the building and the heater never worked. Officer Harrison smoked frantically, puffing deep breaths to get his morning fix, his face turned purple with the lack of oxygen. Officer Cunningham had given up on scolding him years ago, he figured if he didn't stop when his daughter was born then he'd never stop, nagging him wouldn't change a thing.

Officers Harrison and Cunningham were security guards for Fort Gamboge, both failed the physical entrance exam for the military and were lucky to land a job with an 'Officer' ranking. They were a pair of fools, not too smart and horrifically inept in the physical department. The requirement for pre-trained soldiers was ten sit-ups, ten pushups and twenty squats all performed in front of the squad leader. Harrison's twig-like arms could barely perform one push up and Cunningham's gut got in the way for him to fully sit up without rolling to the side.

Fort Gamboge was built to sort the applications and medical records for the whole Army, consisting of a seven-storey office block, a gatehouse and a few surrounding fields, the army base was a short distance from the training camp at Fort Zaffre, The pair's only excitement came when a delivery of personnel, supplies, or the occasional inspector arrived poking his nose making sure the site was 'tip-top'.

Officer Cunningham, sipped on his coffee, slurping with every mouthful, most wouldn't call it coffee, six heaped spoons of sugar and half a cup of double cream, not milk. Cunningham's uniform held on for dear life, at least two sizes too small, his shirt buttons waved over his gut revealing the off-white vest underneath, dried sweat stains tainted the fabric fibres.

"I reckon we'll get a big delivery of applicants today, I've got a feeling" The scrawny Harrison, chuckling under his breath at the thought whilst desperately hiding the jealousy. Harrison was tall with a thin moustache, his skin was pale and sickly. Harrison wore a maroon beanie hat that covered his bald head.

The pair of officers sat at the gatehouse, watching the front drive in anticipation. A twelve-hour shift consisted of sitting in the same chair, eyes locked on the Fort entrance, checking the number plate on vehicles approaching and operating the gate, a tricky operation of pressing the green button for up and the red button for down.

"Bang on time!" Shouted the portly Cunningham, looking at his ironic smart fitness watch.

As usual, a white Double-cab Ford Transit van barreled around the corner at top speed, the driver was a short stocky woman, her hair was grey and curly and she had a permanent scowl etched on her face, she was a grumpy old bat who had been delivering applications since the program began.

The driver was known to the guards as Granny, a fitting title given her appearance and the fact that she had been doing this job for an exceptionally long time.

"Boys!" Granny shouted in a croaky voice, her throat hoarse from a lifetime of alcohol, an unnerving habit for a delivery driver.

"Morning Ma'am!" They replied in unison, the pair of them saluted militarily, the chubby Cunningham wobbled and nearly lost his balance, the two officers looked at each other and giggled like a pair of school girls.

"You boys are fucking ridiculous." Granny chuckled, as she jumped down from the van, she landed with a thud and made her way around the back.

"I'll give you a hand!" Cunningham announced, his chubby face full of excitement, he loved any excuse to get away from his post and away from that awful smell.

"Sure," Granny replied, she wasn't one for social interaction, she would much rather get the job done and head home for a Leidenshire Cocktail, A homemade drink consisting of Whiskey, Gin, and a small dash of Port, all alcohol and no mixer, created for one purpose, getting drunk as fast as possible.

The two opened the back doors and loaded the applications onto a trolley, a lot more than usual, this was a good sign.

"Ha ha, knew it!" Harrison observed. Leaning out the gatehouse window, his elbows pressed on the window sill as he ducked under the fixed glass above his head.

"Mmmm" Granny replied growling to herself, her hatred of the Army was justified, her husband was a career soldier and when he died, the Army wiggled their way through legal loopholes and found the pension plan was 'inconclusive' and should be absorbed by the state. Granny was left with nothing and had to work full-time through her twilight years.

Cunningham wheeled the trolley up the ramp, the squeaky wheels screeched with every turn.

"Thank you Ma'am" Harrison saluted for a second time. Granny nodded in appreciation, as she closed the van doors and took a step back to gain momentum, with a grunt she pushed herself into the driver's seat and started the engine,

"Boys!" She shouted out the window, waving with a crooked smile before reaching for a clear plastic bottle with the label ripped off and swigged the remains of the murky reddish brown drink. Harrison looked stunned.

"Thanks Granny! Have a nice day." The pair replied, they both returned a friendly wave.

Granny reversed the van and headed out, leaving the Officers alone once again, The puff of burnt diesel made Cunningham queasy, that was the last thing he needed.

"I'll get these inside," Cunningham said, choking on his breath, pushing the trolley up the driveway, he huffed and puffed, his face a bright shade of red as beads of sweat formed on his forehead.

"Need a hand there buddy?" Harrison teased, taking another drag of his cigarette.

"Fuck off, I'm fine." Cunningham huffed.

"Suit yourself," Harrison said facetiously.

Cunningham continued up the driveway, the concrete was smooth and flat and the trolley made no trouble rolling up.

Once Cunningham reached the top he balled his fist tight and banged on the steel green door three times, it was an odd custom, but a tradition nonetheless. Cunningham walked gingerly back down the ramp and slumped himself

9

back into his chair, out of breath he sighed as he slammed his feet on the corner of the desk.

Harrison rolled his eyes and flicked the cigarette butt out the window, adding to the small pile, heaped on the grass verge outside. The green door unlocked with a clang and creaked open.

"Mornin" A tall figure greeted them.

"Morning Sergeant," Cunningham replied.

"Looks like a busy day, eh?" Harrison added.

"So it does. Thank the lord." Sergeant Murphy was an older gentleman, in his late 70's, his grey hair was short and neat and he had a large moustache that hid his top lip. Tall, dark and handsome, nobody would ever guess he was 76, still a ladies man he loved to flirt with the ladies at the local bar, telling them tall tales of his time in service.

Murphy opened the gates wide, allowing the trolly through, he grabbed hold of the handle and slowly trudged into the building.

Murphy's job was to transport the applications from the front entrance to the offices, Each floor was built to an exact specification, a wide open space with 'L' shape desks strategically placed to optimise space and flow of foot traffic. A large office at the end of the room for higher ranking officers a segregated area for vending machines and a small kitchenette. The Army never wasted funding, which meant the building's decor was a little bland, to say the least, with white walls, basic man-made wooden desks, and a small notice board for dates in the future. Swivel chairs with worn maroon sponge backing tucked neatly under tables

Every day Murphy would slowly push the trolley up to each line of desks, separate the forms into piles of twenty and move on to the next, and the next, and the next.

The building was mostly empty, there were a couple of cleaning staff on their way home, A few interns keen to show initiative and a few night guards making their last rounds. It was all routine, all boring.

"Morning Sergeant." Said a middle-aged woman with a kind smile, her pristine military uniform framed her curvy physique with dark brown hair tied up in a bun and her face clear of any imperfections she waited for Murphy's response

"Morning Catalina"

Catalina had worked for the program for a little under a decade, the greatest asset to the team, she was a real hard worker.

Catalina grabbed the trolley and began taking the applications to her station, her short black heels tapped rhythmically on the 'well-used' khaki office carpet, there were at least 50 applications in her bundle, which was light work for her.

"Thank you, Sergeant." She said with a smile, the Sergeant tipped his grey tweed flat cap and made his way to the next floor, his eyes closed for a second as he noticed her perfume, delicate notes of honeysuckle and vetiver .

Catalina's olive skin shone like gold and her eyes sparkled like emeralds, she was an exotic beauty. Many brave men had asked her out, all of which were refused, she wasn't interested in men that way.

She was an incredibly hard working lady, her job was to sift through the applications and pass the good ones to the boss, the rest would be passed on to processing.

Processing was the military's way of saying 'You've scraped the barrel of acceptance so we'll drop you in at the deep end and run you through the full training package to see if you had the guts to continue' Nobody wanted to be 'processed'

Slamming the pile of applications on her desk, Catalina sat in her swivel chair and took a sip of her coffee, a strong espresso was just the thing to get the job done, the total opposite of the dessert Cunningham 'brewed' daily. Scooting herself towards the desk, Catalina cracked her neck left and right before flipping the first applicants' folder open,

"Let's see."

Catalina scanned through the documents, skipping the basic info, her eyes searched the cards for anything worthwhile, so far the pickings were slim.

"Hmmm" She said to herself.

"Ah!"

The next applicant seemed interesting, Jasmine, 19 years old, a gymnast in her early teens, an excellent swimmer, top of her class.

"Looks like a perfect recruit to me" Catalina whispered to herself, a smile curled on her rosewood lips as she nibbled the end of her pen, "the boss would definitely be interested in this one."

Catalina placed the application into her green tray, that's where the applications went for consideration, if the boss liked the sound of the applicant then she would take it further.

"Done." She exclaimed.

A little tired Catalina stood up and stretched her back, a satisfying pop rang through her spine, the pain eased and Catalina was ready to go again, she took the first 3 out of the green tray and proceeded down the hallway.

The morning had gone by rather quickly, beams of sunlight shone through the external windows into the office building, like a spotlight on a stage, the warmth was comforting.

Catalina walked towards Lt Gen Anna Isaac's office, she was one of the best officers the SEAL's had ever produced, Retired from the field but still served as head of recruitment for the Army. Catalina tapped twice on the thick wooden door frame with the knuckle of her middle finger. Gold lettering spelled out 'Lt Gen Anna Issac' on the frosted glass.

"Come in." The commanding voice from inside said.

Catalina walked in, papers neatly stacked in her hands.

"What do you have for me?" the Lt General said without looking up.

"Three for consideration Ma'am."

The office was spacious, the walls were lined with bookshelves that reached the ceiling, the room was well kept and tidy, not a speck of dust or dirt anywhere.

A breathtaking view of the city in the distance filled the feature wall. One single pane of glass, ten feet wide and seven feet tall, the sun flooded the room. A Bespoke African Blackwood desk was commissioned for the Lt General as a gift from her superiors, the President of the Republic and the Joint Chief of Staff. The complex design was inspired by the shape and the structure of the Blackwood tree.

The Lieutenant fixed on reading a passage from the book in her hand.

"Okay." the Lt General replied.

She was an intimidating woman, at 6ft tall with broad square shoulders, she towered over most men, A short dark buzz cut and a permanent stern look on her face, even when she smiled, a smile that only those who had known her for a long time knew, to everyone else, it was just a slight upturn at the corners of her mouth.

The lieutenant put down her book and motioned to the seat opposite her.

Catalina sat, she could not help but feel tiny, even though she wasn't short herself, she felt small sitting opposite the lieutenant.

"So, who have you got for me?" the Lt General said, leaning over her desk and steepling her hands, her elbows resting on the armrests. Catalina placed the forms on the table and swivelled them to face the Lieutenant.

"This first one, excellent test results, top of his class," She said pointing at the profile picture.

"A Farmer? Hmph!" the Lt General said with a curious, yet dismissive tone.

"Nineteen and aced the physical...beat your record on the target practice" Catalina said matter-of-factly.

"Interesting," The lieutenant said, folding her arms and leaning back in her chair.

Saint Morgan

My Sweet Love

Oh, my love, my heart's sweetest delight,
In your eyes, my soul takes flight.
Your touch ignites a fire so bright,
My love for you, a shining light.

Your voice, a melody so pure,
My heart beats fast, my love so sure.
In your arms, I find my peace,
My love for you, my heart's release.

I will miss you, my love, so dear,
When we part, my heart will fear.
But I know, my love will remain,
Forever in my heart, a sweet refrain.

"Rounds two and three are his, we got ground to cover but we can still win" Coach Adkins bellowed instructions, his forehead pressed against mine, our noses millimetres from touching. I sat on a stool catching my breath, the air was thick like cream, I choked on every inhale. The cutman pressed a q-tip hard into a cut below my left eye, the sharp sting shot right to the back of my eyeball, and I winced. "Stay fucking focused" Adkins yelled, and slapped the side of my head. I looked up, and nodded, it was the knock back to reality I needed. The bell was going to ring soon, the next round would be mine, I knew it, I trained too hard for this, that was the moment that would determine the rest of my life, So I thought. Winning this fight meant going to regionals and maybe I could make a career of it.

"You can win this" Adkins yelled in my face, I could smell the sour smell of cigar smoke and vodka on his breath. "You can win this," he repeated. My opponent, a twenty-four-year-old Irish-Catholic from Philadelphia named Patrick Maloney. Maloney's undefeated record was impressive and a little intimidating.

"Maloney drops his guard just before he swings a right hook, pop a right jab to throw him off and go for a single leg take-down, your wrestling is better than his" Adkins screamed. I nodded and jumped to my feet as the bell rang and my team cleared the ring, the crowd roared, and I ran to the centre of the ring, my mind focused on Coach's words, the rest was just static noise.

Patrick was a tall opponent, six-foot-two and 135 pounds, all lean muscle, with long legs. He wore his blonde hair in a crew-cut and had a long, thin face. At five-foot-Seven, and 142 pounds, I was shorter than Patrick, but stronger, power was on my side, but he had speed and reach. We bumped gloves and circled around the ring, the crowd chanted our names in turn, I blocked out the sound, and focused on the movements of his body, and the placement of his feet, he crossed his clockwise, I followed in turn. Patrick came at me with a right hook, just like the coach said. I threw a right jab and popped him in the mouth. It threw him off as he stumbled backwards, he dropped his left shoulder. I dove at his legs, and pulled him to the mat. Patrick struggled, I punched him in the kidneys and moved for a ground and pound, Patrick held me in full guard and tightened the position. I punched him in the face, right, left, right, right. In hindsight I see my mistake…gassed too early, the last punch was a mistake. Patrick grabbed my arm, and locked his legs around my neck. He had me in an arm bar and it was tight. I pulled back and tried to stand, but he was strong and his hold was unbreakable. I had a choice to make, tap out, or the arm breaks.

"Tap, damn it, tap" Adkins was screaming. My arm began to tingle, the lack of blood left my arm numb. My elbow and shoulder was under so much stress, I was seconds from a break, the world was getting darker, and I felt myself slipping, I tapped my hand against his chest. The fight was over.

I stood up, and walked toward the ring's edge. I saw Adkins standing there, and he had the biggest grin on his face. "It's all good" he said, and put his hand on my shoulder, he leaned in close.

"We learn from our losses, and grow to be better" he whispered, and then he smiled, pulled the towel from his shoulder, and handed it to me.

"Go clean up, let's get some food" he said, I nodded, and took the towel, walking to the locker room, my legs were wobbly, and my muscles ached. The adrenaline was starting to fade, the pain was creeping in. My arm was heavy, swollen and red, but there was no break, the joint was still intact. Exhausted from the fight I staggered, it felt like a freight train had hit me, maybe the fight game wasn't for me. Thoughts of that nature always ran through my mind after a loss, It was just one of those things, part of the job.

"Hey, Sebastian!" Maloney shouted over to me, trying to get my attention. He was sitting on the floor, the cutman was working on his eye, his coach rubbed liniment into his shoulders. A mix of peppermint and orange filled my nose, his coach used way too much of that stuff, the menthol burn opened my sinuses.

"Yeah" I said, and turned toward him.

"Good fight" Maloney stood up and walked over to me, his arm extended for a handshake. I admired a fighter that could separate the ferocity of the ring to the civility of the outside world, afterall it was a sport, not warfare.

"You too, you have a hell of a hook" Maloney grabbed his chin and attempted to ease the pain.

"That ground and pound would've had me down for quite some time" Maloney said, he smiled at me, and slapped my shoulder.

"Thanks, man," I said.

"Don't beat yourself up about this one, we all take hits, and it's hard, but it's part of the game" Maloney said, before heading to the locker room, He was right, a loss was inevitable, now was not the time to dwell on the fight, time to hit the bags and train, I needed to be better, get a few wins on my record.

Days after the fight flew by, filled with creaky bones and throbbing joints. I felt like shit. I could still taste the blood, the sticky metallic taste lingerd. I was so tired, Natasha stayed with me the whole time. It's hard for me to explain just how much she was a part of my life and how much I loved her, she was my everything.

It was a long week of recovery and painkillers, but finally I started to feel like myself again. It's funny, Natasha supported my MMA, she watched every fight from the sidelines, she hated the losses more than me. The only time I saw her angry was when the ref raised the opponent's arm.

"C'mon lets get out of the house, get some fresh air, Milo misses the creek" she smiled. She knew what she was doing *'Milo misses the creek'* yea sure, use the dog. Natasha loved the creek, to be fair, so did I.

The place she had in mind was the same place we shared our first kiss. The memories that flooded back every time we arrived at our spot. Crazy how memories can fill your heart and break it at the same time.

Milo sat on the same patch of grass beside the riverbank, he spent hours staring at the yellow perch, too old to catch any, he'd just watch them swimming by, some would pluck up the courage to kick up water splashing Milo on the nose, It made Natasha giggle every time. Milo was my first dog, a chocolate labrador, daft old thing. He'd play in muddy puddles and bury himself in filth everytime we went out. Somehow he loved it, it was the best part of our walks together, watching his fat belly barrel down the dirt track, panting like crazy as he found a thick boggy puddle. Beams of sunlight poked through the tall redwood branches as they swayed in the summer breeze. Saint Morgan's bakery was a five minute walk away, the smell of toasted oats and sweet honey would blow over the riverbank straight into our treehouse. Every Sunday morning we would watch as the townspeople lined up in a long, neat queue, their pockets jingling with change. Sometimes we'd join them, waiting in anticipation for the front doors to open. The first few people in line would leave carrying large bags, and I would imagine what kind of treats were inside. When we got to the front of the line, we would order the same thing: A six pack of Madeleines, two cinnamon cappuccinos and two giant croissants, the lady would always throw in a couple treats for Milo, cheesy bacon puffs, perfect for our 'gutso'.

23

The coffees would keep us warm right through till late in the evening. The treehouse was our home away from home, we spent years perfecting the build, Natasha's Uncle worked at the lumber yard and always gave us the month's offcuts, it was perfect for us. The small porch led to the deck which overlooked the riverbank, the moss-covered roof kept the whole structure waterproof. Nobody ventured into our part of the forest, it was our secret spot. Natasha played her steel-stringed pinewood, Gibson, her father had stained it to a cherry red, her favourite colour. The sound had a sweet, yet sharp twang to it, a twang that echoed through trees, her voice was breathtaking, soft with that slight country crack at the end of her notes, Perfection. She played an old Tracy Jackman song, "My Sweet Love"

We'd sometimes lay in the grass, looking up at the sky, making crazy stories about the cloud creatures that would float by, we'd sometimes find shapes of things we could see, like spaceships with sky pirates. The clouds would turn a deep shade of orange as the sun would sink down. The fireflies were bright against the backdrop of a deep blue and black sky, and the fire before us, kept us warm, it gave off the perfect ambiance.

"Milo, let's go."

Milo slowly peaked one eye open as if he didn't quite hear me and pretended to be asleep,

"Milo! C'mon old boy. Home Time"

Milo never needed a leash, loyal and obedient, the greatest dog, I couldn't ask for more. He'd sit and wait by the truck while we took our last few glances at the night sky, deep shades of purple mixing and fading with the clouds, playing peek-a-boo with the stars as they twinkled from afar.

The ride home was quiet, we were both tired, the days we spent there were some of the best days of my life, I can still remember the feeling of pure bliss I felt when I could sit and stare into Natasha's eyes, I'd smile and think about how perfect everything was. The long road home curved and banked around the whole town, passing the familiar landmarks we saw daily. Saint Morgan was a tiny place, nothing too spectacular about it. The population was less than a thousand, everyone was close, a friendly town, it had a sense of security. Sometimes it really got on Natasha's nerves, everyone knowing our business and poking their nose where it didn't belong. People just needed something to interest in, it just so happened the local gossip kept their simple minds occupied.

We arrived at Natasha's house first, her folks were honest hard workers, her mother was a nurse, at four foot nine Lily reached on her tiptoes to hug Natasha, she always wore her nurse scrubs and had her hair tied in a bun, I never saw her without lipstick on. Natasha's mother was the only person to call me Sebby, everyone else called me Sebastian. It was a special bond we had, more like a mother than a future mother-in-law.

"Eesh Sebby, look at your face, baby, why do you do this?" She ran down the porch steps and grabbed my face as I sat in the car, with the window down, the engine slowly purred as it sat in neutral. She looked at the cuts and bruises from the previous fight.

"Oh Ma, stop embarrassing him," Natasha shouted from the front door

"Sebby, you have to stop this MMA nonsense, you have such a handsome face" She cupped my chin with her hands and smiled, she knew MMA was a part of me and that I was never going to quit.

Natasha's father was a cop, stern but fair, Officer William Miller always stood with his back flexed and his chest puffed out, his old fashioned cop-stash was perfectly trimmed, I suppose it was all part of the 'look', a figure of authority, It worked. Natasha was an only child, Obviously this meant she was the light of their world, they spoiled her rotten and they would give anything for her happiness.

Every night I'd follow Natasha up the front steps to the porch, kiss her goodnight and say goodbye to her folks before I headed home. I loved her and her family, they made me a part of their family and they always welcomed me. They loved the fact that we were so close, the whole town kinda knew we'd be together forever, something about giving them 'yummy vibes' whatever that meant.

When I wasn't in the ring or training in the gym, I worked on the farm about five minute walk from Natasha's house, looking after the animals and the land was hard work but it kept me honest. The owners of the land let me set up in the small guest house, it was a perfect deal for me, I got a place to live, a paycheck and the animals were great company for me and Milo. Mr and Mrs Kinsley were good people, they were retired and had a passion for growing fruits and vegetables, their farm was well known and the produce sold well to the locals. Their son had adopted a big city life, so they left it all to me to run.

Post was delivered at 7:52 sharp everyday, Mr Waterson was the postman, he never changed his time by a minute. I could set my clock by him, he was as reliable as the day was long. "Morning, Sebastian" he called as he walked past the barn, I was feeding the cows, I poked my head up like a meerkat. His uniform was crisp and freshly ironed, a pale blue button up shirt and navy chino shorts, he looked sharp and the fit complemented his muscular physique.

"Mornin" I replied and gave a friendly nod.

"Got a letter from Fort Gamboge, got an urgent stamp on the envelope buddy" he continued.

My heart sank.

"That's my draft notice isn't it" I said more as a statement than a question. My heart pounded so hard I could feel the beat in my ears.

He nodded slowly, "Probably"

I walked towards him and took the letter from his hand, he gave me a sympathetic pat on the back.

"Good luck Sebastian" he carried on with his round.

I opened the envelope and pulled out the letter.

'To Sebastian Moretti,

You have been drafted and are required to report to the nearest military barracks within 72 hours of receiving this letter.

Your recent results from the physical aptitude tests have been brought to our attention, we'd like to offer you an exciting position in the newly developed Sector C Special Operations.

You are to be congratulated on this opportunity to attend the military academy, for it comes only to a select few. It presents a challenge that will demand your best effort.

Sincerely yours

Lt General Anna Isaac

I put the letter down and took a deep breath.

It's happening. Thoughts ran through my mind and the farm began to spin, I sat down and calmed my nerves.

My whole life, all I had known, had been on the farm, living the country-boy life. I had no idea how to be a soldier. I looked at Milo.

"Looks like you're living with Natasha buddy" I smiled sympathetically at his daft old face, he didn't have a clue but gave this sad soft 'sulky' face, I laughed and rubbed his head.

"Don't worry buddy,"

I walked out of the barn, closing the gate behind me, I sat down on a log and read the letter again, by this time the breeze had slowly dried the panic sweat from my forehead and my heart slowed down to an acceptable pace.

"This could be a good thing" I told myself.

"Or a very bad thing" I thought.

I decided to tell Natasha at dinner, I couldn't bear telling her and her folks separately, just get it over with. The day dragged, every minute felt like an hour, 19:00 every Sunday was a tradition at the Everly household, A Turkey roast with all the trimmings. My stomach growled with hunger, I hadn't eaten all day, Lily's cooking was amazing, a real treat, but the thought of my upcoming departure made the food taste like ash in my mouth.

The house was full of laughter and the clinking of cutlery against china plates, Natasha sat opposite me at the table, she wore a beautiful summer dress that accentuated her curves, she smiled at me, her eyes bright and twinkling with love, her hair fell down to her shoulders, the settling sun from the window behind her illuminated her features and highlighted her beauty.

Natasha's parents sat beside us, chatting about the day and how much the farm was thriving.

"I can't congratulate you enough, son." Natasha's father said, raising his glass to me. "The Kinsley business is booming, people have been talking"

"It's all because of your daughter, Mr Miller, it's her ideas that have led to the business becoming so successful" I said, glancing at Natasha, I reached over and squeezed her hand gently.

I sat there, my palms sweaty, I tried to swallow the lump that had formed in my throat.

I couldn't bring myself to speak, the words just wouldn't come out.

"Sebastian, honey are you okay?" Lily asked with concern in her voice.

I shook my head and reached for the letter in my back pocket, I held it out, Natasha took it and her mother read it over her shoulder.

"Oh no, no this can't be happening" Lily's eyes welled with tears she launched at me, almost knocking me off my chair, her arms wrapped around me and squeezed tight.

"When do you leave?" Natasha asked, her eyes filled with tears, her cheeks blushed rosy and her voice squeaked.

I paused apprehensively I didn't want to reply "Tomorrow"

Natasha began to sob falling into my arms, I held her tight and let her cry, she struggled to catch her breath.

"Sebastian, we're gonna miss you so much, it's gonna be so quiet around here without you, son," Natasha's father said solemnly.

"Yes sir" I sighed.

I took a deep breath.

"Nat, you know I'll write to you every chance I get and I'll come home as soon as I can. You are the love of my life, we're gonna be married and start our own family and we'll grow old together, I promise." I said, unsure if I was lying.

She hugged me tighter, I could barely breathe

"I love you," she sobbed.

"I love you too, Nat"

We stayed up until the early hours, staring at the logs, crackling in the fireplace, each knot snapping like bubble wrap. The flames held our attention, words couldn't help the situation, we just spent what little time we had cuddled up under old blankets hugging warm cups of hot chocolate.

"Let's go for a walk," Natasha said suddenly.

The fire made me drowsy but the moment those words left her lips, I knew what I wanted.

Natasha and I went for a walk along the dirt path that led to the Treehouse, Milo led the way. We didn't say a word, her head lay on my shoulder and our fingers locked tight.

The moon shone brightly over the water, ripples of silvery light spreading in every direction. The breeze was warm and carried the scent of the apple orchards.

I climbed the ladder, then turned and took Natasha's hand. I unpacked a thick duvet and hugged it tight around the both of us, Milo sat guard at the bottom.

Natasha snuggled into my arms and we lay back, looking up at the stars, a tear rolled down my cheek and landed on her hair. She looked up and wiped the second droplet away before kissing my cheek, her body pressed against mine, her lips were soft and tender, she slowly found mine, our kiss was passionate and deep, as if she was afraid this was her only chance to kiss me, our tongues explored each other, tasting each other, dancing and caressing.

Natasha's touch was soft, her fingers trailed across my chest and she kissed my neck. I was still dazed and confused about everything, but at the same time, my body was alive and craving more of Natasha's touch.

"I'll be with you, Sebastian, forever" she whispered.

Her cheeks flushed. She looked into my eyes, and we made love under the stars.

We stayed there until the sun rose and the birds sang their morning songs. It was beautiful and romantic. As the sky grew lighter, and the first rays of light broke through the forest, we slowly got dressed.

It was time to go. We packed up and took one last look at the treehouse. The walk back took twice as long. We made each last second together count. As we arrived at Natasha's house, I looked at Milo, he looked back obliviously.

"You're the best dog, Milo" I said, kneeling down, ruffling his head, he took the opportunity and went for one big sloppy lick, chin to nose. "Ok, cheers pal" I giggled and scratched under his chin.

"I'll look after him, I promise" Taking the opportunity whilst kneeling, Lily kissed me on the forehead. "Now, off with you, before I start crying again"

I headed over to the farmhouse to lock up and grab my rucksack, an old GMC Sierra pickup truck was parked in the driveway waiting for me. It was Coach Adkins, he stood there chewing on sunflower seeds, spitting the shells into the neighbour's bush

."I heard the news kid"

He walked over to me as I approached the front porch

"Yea," I looked down, I should've told him myself "Got the letter yesterday"

"I know." Coach placed his hand on my shoulder and squeezed. "It's been a pleasure coaching you."

"Thanks coach" I looked up at him, he had a faint hint of tears in his eyes, before I could say anything else he walked around his truck and jumped into the driver's seat, the loud clack and bang broke the tension, a large puff of black smoke flew from the exhaust.

 "Let me know when you're back, we'll get a session in"

The comment was a little weird, to think I'd train MMA on my rare days home was odd to say the least, but the coach was like that, focused on the fight game, and only the fight game

I packed the house and laid sheets over the furniture, with nobody home. I wanted to leave the place in good condition. As I closed the door, something caught my eye.

Mr Kinsley's rifle sat in the corner, I never knew why he kept it, he wasn't the hunting type, it was more of an ornament. I took it down and examined it, it was heavy, the stock was comfortable and fit my grip perfectly.

A wave of emotion swept over me. I couldn't explain it, my senses heightened, my breathing was slow and steady, my fingers brushed mahogany body and gripped the trigger. I checked the weapon and pulled the sight to my right eye, closing the left. I knew the war would change me, this was the first step.

Natasha waited outside, her cheeks still damp from crying. I could see the pain in her face. There was no need for her to say anything.

I loaded the truck, and sat in the driver's seat, Natasha jumped into the passenger seat and held my hand tight,

"Ready?" she asked.

I nodded and we drove off.

The drive was the longest I had ever taken. Natasha's hand was clutched in mine the whole time, not once did she let go. We normally played country music obnoxiously loud, singing along to the words, making a fool of ourselves. It didn't seem right this time.

The sign 'Fort Zaffre next left' made Natasha take a deep breath, she looked at me and smiled.

The gates of the military academy were intimidating, tall and black, they had 'No Unauthorised Access' printed on the side.

Natasha hugged me tight and I jumped out of the truck, I grabbed my bag leaving the engine running, Natasha shuffled over to the driver's seat, she didn't want to see the actual enlistment process, but I understood.

"I'll write you a letter every day," she said through the open window.

I nodded and waved as she circled the truck and drove off.

I watched her go, and stood alone. The soft sweet smell of cinnamon madeleine, Cappuccinos and Natasha's wild jasmine and lily perfume slowly faded. The foul odour of boot polish and gunpowder struck a nerve, I screwed my face in shock, the stench only got stronger.

A soldier approached and saluted, his military boots clacked and slammed the ground, I saluted back, admittedly a little clumsy and light on my feet, he gestured me towards the Fort entrance, the giant gate towered over me, at least twenty feet tall with barbed wire coiling the top, was it to keep unwanted visitors out or soldiers in? I wasn't sure.

"Lt Gen Anna Isaac is waiting" He barked out sentences with little emotion, he didn't even look at me.

My whole life had changed in the space of a week, now was the time to become a man, a soldier, a member of the Dark Watch.

Fort Zaffre

Secret Hideouts

In a secret hideout, hidden from view
Where the world cannot find us, we'll train anew
A place to hone our skills, to test our might
And become the heroes, of this endless fight

The hideout's walls, they whisper secrets old
Of spells and magic, that the world has never told
The trees that surround us, they whisper too
Of ancient wisdom, that only they knew

The river that runs, it whispers of the sea
The creatures that dwell, in its depths, you'll see
The wind that blows, it carries the scent
Of adventure and danger, and the thrill of the hunt

I took a deep breath and walked forward, without sign or notice the gate opened, the weight of the structure dragged a deep trench into the dirt, a fresh scar on a smooth surface, this was the first time the gate had opened, at least for a long time. It was everything I had imagined, soldiers running laps around a large field with drill sergeants yelling instructions. Soldiers in military garb of tan t-shirts and boots with green camouflage trousers. The rhythmic stomp of their feet pounding the ground reminded me of the crowds at the Octagon, crazed, bloodthirsty fans demanding violence, it felt like home. I passed the threshold and everything changed. Like stepping through a layer of jelly, my body tossed and wobbled. It was clearly an illusion. The heavy gate slammed shut behind me, pushing me forward.

The alarming contrast of the illusion startled me, dull and monochromatic, Ironic really for a name like Zaffre. I looked down and noticed a strange black sand. I crouched down and rubbed the tips of my fingers across the grainy material, the handful of sand poured from my fist, it felt cool and slightly sticky. Was it some sort of magical spell on the Fort? I hadn't seen anything like it.

I looked around, and realised that it wasn't just the sand that was black, it was everywhere, like a blanket of emptiness and sorrow dragging reality to doom and regret. The ground outside Fort Zaffre was lush and teeming with life. Fields of golden wheat, trees towering over the road providing shade, the wild flowers grew with bright vivid colours. A stark contrast to the death and decay inside the high walls. The smell of rotten flesh made me gag, sour and putrid with undertones of ammonia.

There was an eerie vacuum of sound, as if the whole world was holding its breath, the deafening silence, unbearable. I felt a slight breeze pass by my shoulder, the faint sound of laughter broke the silence, it wasn't a sharp cackle, more like a warming baritone from a familiar friend. I had no idea where I was, but I knew I was far from the safety of Saint Morgan.

An interrupting bellow from across the Fort screamed my name. It shook the entire place, like a tremor from the depths underground, the raw power erupted at my feet.

"Moretti!"

My body snapped to attention, my heart rate rocketed, sweat began to drip down the back of my neck, and the feeling of panic and terror rose and gripped my throat, choking me, the voice was so domineering and demanding.

"Yes Sir?" my words seeped out like a whispering dog

The menacing figure approached with ferocity, his stature was enormous, and muscles from unnatural places bulged in anger. By the badges and his demeanour, I could tell he was of higher ranking. He stormed from the exercise equipment tucked in the corner of the courtyard, the clanging of weight plates crashed and clattered.

"The Lt General needs to speak with you, don't keep her waiting!"

I nodded, "Of course sir"

My legs were stiff and my arms felt like lead weights, I could barely walk without tripping. I looked down and noticed that my hands were trembling so fast I couldn't focus on the shape, a blurry mess of digits.

"Get a grip" I whispered to myself. One step at a time I moved my body forward towards the front entrance of the building. Over the black sand I staggered leaving long drag marks behind me, I can still remember the intimidating architecture, gothic victorian coves arched over the doorway and rose to the sky.

I arrived about ten feet away from the door, my palms were clammy yet cold to the touch, as I took a deep breath to calm my nerves, a wave of warm, humid air and the sweet smell of coffee washed over me, it was such a contrast to the smell of death and decay outside. The front door swung open to the interior of Lt General's office.

The Lt General was sitting behind her desk, her uniform pristine and sharp, boots polished like mirrors, she sat poised, focused on the doorway, straight at me. I was surprised to see that her hair was buzzed short. It was an old fashioned tradition to militarise a soldier's haircut in order to adhere to a uniform, it apparently gave off the 'One Unit' vibe. She gestured for me to sit opposite her. I looked at the two empty chairs and chose the one that was closest to the exit, as I sat down the other chair crumbled into dust. Everything that day made me second guess my decisions, my instincts were questioned, what would have happened if I chose the other chair?

"Moretti?"

"Yes Ma'am"

She could see the fear in my eyes. She broke the tension and smiled, the corners of her lips broke, creases in her cheeks formed yet her eyes stayed cold and sharp, focused on my every move. Clearly a tactic to manipulate the room, lure me into a false sense of security, what for? To this day, I'm still not sure.

"At ease" Her voice was sultry and creamy, her thick British accent rolled off her tongue.

"Yes Ma'am,"

She sighed and leaned back, her eyes scanning me from head to toe.

"I'm guessing you know the purpose of this war?"

"I'm sorry, no I don't Ma'am."

She raised an eyebrow,

"So you haven't been paying attention?"

I shrugged, clueless

"No one speaks of the war, we just accept it as the norm, Ma'am"

She laughed and then shook her head in a disappointed manner. It was clear she hated my blind ignorance.

"Nothing normal about this," She leaned back and folded her arms "Nothing normal at all"

I nodded, having no idea what she was talking about, I was desperate not to make a fool of myself, to make sure I fell in line and did what was asked. Maybe If I served well, made a good impression, I could go home early with one or two tours on my belt.

She stood up and walked around the desk, leaning against the front of it,

"Your testing was a part of your education at Evergreen Grammar School?"

"Yes Ma'am."

"Your cognitive aptitude tests are impressive" the Lt flicked through a stack of paperwork "Impressive MMA record too"

"Thank you Ma'am"

"But what's most important is that your results were better than mine at your age. High levels of Dopamine and Cortisol, 150 on your aptitude test and 740 in awareness."

"Is that good Ma'am?"

"It's perfect, best I've seen"

"For what?"

She smiled and stared into my eyes. I could tell she was contemplating the situation in her head, a back and forth process of weighing the odds to calculate my worth.

"I'm putting you forward for Sector C Spec ops"

I sat there, frozen and unsure how to react.

"I have selected the very best soldiers from each regimen. You should feel honoured, not only have you been accepted into the Dark Watch, but you've been accepted into Spec ops! You'll be trained in counter-insurgency, guerilla warfare and intelligence gathering. Not to mention....enhanced augmentation"

"What is that, Ma'am?"

"It will make you stronger, faster and more lethal. Your senses will be enhanced, and you will be the very best of the best. But, you will need to work as a team, Sector C will be your new family"

I stood up and saluted,

"Thank you, Lt General."

She held my gaze, her expression was blank, her eyes were cold and calculating. She was a master manipulator with a keen sense of emotional intelligence. Lt Gen Issac gave nothing away that day.

"This is an elite group, you will need to work harder and faster than any other recruit. We will break you, then build you up, stronger and more lethal."

I gulped,

"Yes Ma'am, when do I start?"

She stood and walked over to the door, she looked at me and reached for the handle, pulling the door towards her.

"Right now!"

It took me a second to realise, I was a little naive and green back then. Lt General had a spell on Fort Zaffre, the doorway would teleport to wherever she needed. As I stepped out, Lt General was gone.

Triple bunk beds lined both walls, four stacks on each side. Cream tiled floor and navy blue walls, the place was spotless. Each bed was folded and pressed to perfection, not a crease in sight. The whole place smelled of cleaning products and polish. A faint sound of laughter came from beyond the room.

"Moretti? Welcome to the Spec Ops"

I turned to see a tall, blonde woman standing behind me, she reached out her hand.

"My name is Sergeant Ackerman, you can call me Sarge."

I shook her hand and nodded, I was still disoriented by the teleportation doorway. It was all new to me, spells and teleportations, enhanced augmentations and guerilla warfare were all terms that a boy from the county had no business knowing.

"Nice to meet you Ma'am" her presence was intimidating, not as much as the Lt Gen, but still enough to make me nervous.

Sarge sighed and raised her eyebrow,

"Ma'am? I've looked at your records, Moretti! I'm two years older than you. I'm your CO. You call me Sarge or boss."

I gulped,

"Sarge it is, boss"

She laughed and patted me on the shoulder, her hand felt like a boulder, it physically burdened me, like her fists could ball up into kettlebells at any moment.

"Come on, everyone's out back. They're dying to meet you."

I followed her into the next room, the sheer volume of noise, cheering and yelling. Aggressive tones mixed with bursts of expletives.

"FUCK! Two guards on your left, you need to pass to the right!"

A worn out couch struggled to hold a frantic five man team, dirt spots showed its character, areas that were once mint green, now a stained mish-mash of brown. Years of Chinese food and pizza sauce. The group gathered round the sixty-five inch TV that was bolted on the wall, AC Warriors were playing the Chiefs. The game of TriggerSlam was alien to me. Teams of six would shoot and fight each other in an AI generated environment, like a video game on steroids.

The room went quiet, the game was paused and a tall, skinny guy walked over to me. He had a goofy smile,

"I'm Jameson, you must be Moretti."

I nodded and shook his hand. It dawned on me that nobody used first names here, greeting people as Sebastian was out of the question.

"That's right, nice to meet you Jameson."

"Nice to meet you too. I've heard a lot about you. Big time MMA fighter. This is Munganga, we call her Em. Jameson pointed at a mysterious girl in the corner of the room, she kept herself to herself and barely acknowledged me. He made his way round the room introducing me to the team, the names came thick and fast, it was hard to keep up.

"Which camp are you from?" Jameson asked, trying to bridge a gap, hoping to find common ground.

I looked at him and shrugged,

"Fresh recruit, no training, no...camp, Lt Gen Issac sent me here, from what I assume was Fort Zaffre"

Everyone looked at me in shock, the room went silent, thankfully Jameson was the first to speak,

"You met the Lt General? That's awesome! What's she like? What was she wearing?"

"What the fuck Jameson! You're a sick pervert" Sarge clipped him round the back of his head and scowled, gave him a look, she growled like a demon. "Out of line soldier!"

Jameson rubbed the back of his head and smiled at me before cowering under Sarge's gaze.

"Apologies Sarge"

I shrugged my shoulders trying to buy time to satisfy the room, "Friendly enough, I suppose"

Sarge cleared her throat,

"OK team, listen up. Moretti has basic training and aug tests, let's keep it quiet and have an early one."

A short, stocky girl, with curly red hair, jumped up,

"Ohhhh shit! He's gonna get a taste of the Bisco"

The whole team laughed and began to chat, and the sound of a pinball machine started up, I grabbed two pool cues and threw one to Jameson,

"Wanna play?"

He looked at the cue and nodded,

"You're on"

Sarge and a couple of the others went back to watching the game.

"I'll let you break", Jameson said with a cocky tone

"Oh, you'll regret it!"

The balls cracked and scattered. Jameson watched and smiled,

"Good shot!"

I sunk two more before missing the third by a hair,

"You're pretty good!"

I changed the subject, "So, training? That includes enhanced augmentation?" I was desperate to know my fate, what did it all mean.

Jameson leaned against his cue, his brow furrowed,

"It'll hurt like a bitch, but it's what keeps us all alive"

I nodded, and thought back to what the Lt Gen said,

'Do you guys get sent on missions around the world?'

Jameson jabbed the white into the yellow as it flew into the hole, almost leaving a scorch mark.

"That's the main reason we're here. Spec ops are the very best, an Elite squad, specialised in everything, guerilla warfare, hostage rescue, deep recon. We do it all, but we always work as a team, no matter what."

He missed his shot and shook his head,

"Fuck, looks like you win" he balled his fist and held it in front of him, I followed suit and bumped fists respectfully.

"Thanks for the game, maybe you can try again another time"

"Oh, For sure! I can give you a tour if you want.

I nodded, "That'll be great!"

We spent the next two hours looking round the facility, it was big, much bigger than I'd anticipated. Jameson explained that the base was made especially for us and our...talents.

"Jameson, I need to stop you there" The imposter syndrome kicked in. I felt inadequate and was well aware and fearful of wasting their time.

He turned and looked at me, his eyebrows raised,

"I think there's been a mistake, I don't have any...talents. The Lt General said I was the best recruit she'd ever seen, but I don't know how that's even possible. I'm not spec ops material"

He nodded, smiled and crossed his arms,

"We all individually thought that about ourselves, this time tomorrow ask me that question again" Jameson continued the tour, he felt uncomfortable with answering too many questions.

"So, this is the gym, and through there is the shooting range. Everything we do is designed to prepare us for the next mission"

"What about food?"

"Through there is the mess hall." Jameson pointed across the hall, the double doors led to a dining area much too large for the small team "There is no shortage of food, so feel free to eat as much as you want" Jameson paused and looked at his wristwatch "listen, it's getting late, tomorrow is a huge day for ya and I for one am looking forward to seeing your potential."

I grinned awkwardly, I wasn't sure what he meant by *'seeing my potential'*

"Welcome to the team, I'll see you tomorrow, 06:00" Jameson walked off finishing his sentence with his back turned to me.

"Yeah, 06:00, ok, see you then" I made my way back to the dormatroy as Jameson headed to the common room. I searched for a bunk with an empty footlocker.

"Oh hey, are you looking for a bunk?" The voice came from a small girl, she looked about twelve years old, way too young for the military.

"Yeah, is that an open footlocker?" I pointed at the bunk above the one she was currently in

"Yeah, all yours"

"I guess, if it's not taken" I didn't have anything on me to fill the footlocker, just the clothes on my back.

"It's cool, names Church " She extended her hand and shook mine, an old fashioned handshake from such a young girl was strange, formal. I was expecting a fist bump at least.

"Moretti"

She smiled and continued reading her book 'Heart of Thirst'. I could tell she wasn't like the others, loud and brash, she seemed reserved and introverted, but then again I wasn't any better.

I laid down on the mattress, which felt surprisingly comfortable. It was quiet, but not silent, you could hear people talking in the hall and the sounds of the base outside. My mind was racing, I had joined the army, or rather, Sector C Special Operations, a secret black-ops type unit, day one of the rest of my military career. The day's events took a toll, I was shattered and needed rest, especially for the day ahead.

Stuff of Nightmares

The New Me

My heart beats strong, my soul takes flight,
I soar on eagle's wings tonight.
The world may doubt, but I know,
I'm on a journey, to where I want to go.

A new me, a new dawn, a new start,
I'll dance in the rain, and sing in the sun,
A fresh beginning, a work of art.
I'll chase my dreams, until they're done.

The limbs, once weak and frail, now strong,
With graceful curves and lines, now long,
The flesh, once dull and lacking hue,
Now glows with colours pure and true.

Fort Zaffre sprung to life in the early hours of the morning, If you could call it that. 0400 was still the middle of night in my opinion, but the military thought differently, 'Waking up before the enemy' and 'Early bird wins the war' were just some of the quotes from the brainwashed soldiers. Militarised drones, all fighting for a cause bigger than themselves, never knowing what that cause was.

"Big day Moretti! Rise and shine! Move Move Move!" Sgt Ackerman barged into the dorm like a bull in a china-shop, she barked orders into a mega-phone that ripped through my ear drum, the sound was crackly and gave me an intense throbbing head pain which ran from my ears to right behind my eyes. Sarge held up what looked like a flashlight, the top popped open and spun round like the top of a lighthouse, beams of light raced around the room flooding the area, painfully ending my peaceful slumber. I realised where I was and what she meant by 'Big day', like a jack-in-the-box, I pounced out of bed forgetting I was on top bunk and ended up smacking my head on the ceiling and crashed down, fumbling idiot. I hit the floor with a 'thump' and was met with the laughter of my dorm-mates, they were already up, dressed and had folded their bunks. I stood up, rubbing my head, and glared at Sarge. She stood three centimetres away from my face, the smell of fresh toothpaste burst from her mouth with every word she spoke. She stood proud and waited there holding the megaphone and pointing the light in my face. Intimidation was the game, she held all the cards, chips and pieces.

"Get dressed, your first test is in five minutes!" she yelled through the megaphone before turning on her heel 90 degrees and leaving with the others scuttering behind her. I looked down at my feet and found my combat uniform, black and white camouflage trousers with pockets running down the sides and a grey round neck t-shirt, Black tactical boots sat on top of the pile, clean and polished to perfection. I quickly got changed, the dorm was quiet, and nobody was around. I reckon they were just as keen as I to find out my potential in all this. I could hear them all whispering and gossiping in anticipation. I yanked my boot strings tight with a double knot and tucked my shirt into the waistband, matching the others.

"Deep breath Moretti…Day One" Something about muttering positive affirmations was supposed to be good for you…but this was ridiculous, I had no idea what was ahead, Day One of what?

"Moretti. Do not be alarmed," Sarge looked at me with a guilty look on her face. Maybe she'd realised the 'drill-sergeant' routine was too much and took it down a notch or two.

The room was dim, a single lamp lit the corner and it flickered away like crazy. If an inanimate object could have tourettes, this lamp definitely had it. My eyes struggled to adjust to the pulsing glow. A single wooden chair stood lonely in the middle of the room, splinters stuck out like bladed shards, it was definitely used for torture…but why? The walls were roughly painted a deep shade of red, the paint was old and peeled, large chunks sat in piles of dust and debris on the floor. There were no windows and the floor was concrete with chips missing, to say this room needed a little TLC was a huge understatement, more like a demolition job. The place was cold and eerie, and the ever-so-faint breeze was unnerving, with no windows, the cold air must have been coming from somewhere. I walked over to the chair and sat down, Sarge slammed the door shut behind me and left me alone without any instruction or notice as to what was going to happen. I waited, and I waited. After what felt like forever, a man entered the room, At least eight feet tall he bowed a little as he passed the doorway. Dressed in a pristine three-piece black suit and a black tie, he stood out from the rest of us. His hair was jet black and slicked backwards behind his ears. His stern look clearly depicted a man who didn't take shit from anyone and I for one wasn't going to test him. I wanted out, quickly and without trouble. I was recruited and adhered to every rule, I dropped everything and enlisted the next day, I wanted to serve my country, be a part of something bigger, and do my duties. Thoughts raced through my mind. Was I being tortured by my own countrymen? I had no secrets, nothing to hide. Did I do something wrong? His thick black welder goggles looked so out of place with his formal attire, it was such a dark room too, I realised they were not built for eye protection but more for dramatic effect, It worked. Shadows caressed the features of his face in a harrowing way. The flickering light only illuminated so much. I gazed up at the taller male with a look of pure, consternation. My brows furrowed as he gave me a sly, cunning smile. He knew just how to get what he wanted, and what he wanted was me.

"No, wait..I…" words barely formed in my mouth.

He slowly coiled leather straps over my arms holding me tight to the chair, jolting the buckle to the tightest hole, my limbs went numb from the grip of the bindings. He moved onto my ankles, bolting them to the floor with metal cuffs, I was well and truly trapped. I panicked, the straps were too tight, they dug into my wrists.

"What the hell is going on?" I failed to keep my composure and remember that it was all a test, the straps, the flickering light and the uncomfortable chill all got the better of me. He walked over to the exit and slowly bolted each lock, from top to bottom he rhythmically cranked the door. It was just me and him, alone together, with no witnesses, my breath felt heavy, I gasped for air, it felt like I was drowning. His tall stature towered over me, he whipped off his goggles and revealed large irregular scars that covered his eyes shut, the skin stretched thin and shiny around each of them. How could he see? I had no time to think about that though. He sneered, as if he knew what I was thinking and somehow I offended him, his lip curled away from his yellowed, pincer-like teeth, they grew in odd directions.

"What do you want?" I yelled, the fear of the unknown was too much, my voice wavered and cracked, my throat was sore and dry. His face was inches away from mine. The faint sound of clicking got louder and louder, from a slight whisper to an uncomfortable crank on my sanity, his jaw opened wide and revealed the inside of his mouth, it was dark, almost black, the clicking continued. My eyes widened with fear, I tried to turn away but his hand shot out and gripped my jaw tightly, he squeezed hard, making me gasp for air, as I did he exhaled sharply. Green smoke erupted from his throat and was forced into mine. The heavy thick fog made me gag and swallow, the feeling of cold numbness overtook me, the room slowly sank into darkness.

"Let's get started!" A deep raspy voice whispered, the words were forced into my brain, the feeling of being violated was sickening, like something was crawling in the back of my skull, an itch that couldn't be scratched.

I awoke, still strapped to the chair, my throat was sore, the same feeling after a general anaesthetic, coming round to reality and feeling groggy, the taste of bitter smoke was fresh in my mouth, clammy and sticky like maple syrup without the sweetness. I could still smell the smoke in the air, it lingered and hung like a thick fog, a mix of vomit and ash. The smell was unbearable, especially the thought that it was inside of me.

My bindings fell limp and collapsed to the floor. I looked down at the straps, no sign of tearing or broken clasps, was this real or just a test?

I didn't want to wait around to find out, the man in the suit could be back, maybe this was my chance at escaping. I leapt out of the chair and dashed for the door...Locked, I jiggled the handle a few times before giving up.

"Fuck, now what"

I searched the room and found a crowbar, not the ideal weapon but better than nothing. The door was strong, metal, at least three inches thick, the frame was thicker. Getting a crowbar lodged in enough so I could break it open was near impossible, maybe with the correct application of strength I could pry open the handle. At this point I was desperate, anything was better than staying in that room. I was wrong.

The door gave way and flung open, as if it was all part of the plan, I definitely didn't apply enough pressure, the comforting smell of toasted oats and sweet honey engulfed my senses, thoughts of Saint Morgan's Bakery and our spot on the riverbank flooded my mind, it paralysed me, held in place, I was frozen, Something so pure and innocent was jarring and so unexpected.

I looked up, there she was, her soft skin glowing in the moonlight, the wind blowing through her long blonde hair, her lips glistened, wet from her tongue. She smiled and held her hand out to me.

"Hey handsome, come with me!" Her words were velvet against my skin and her smile made me weak, like the first time I laid my eyes on her. I could have fallen into her arms and stayed forever, she was beautiful, her dress hugged her figure and flowed out at her waist. I was speechless, my throat ran dry, her soft giggle echoed in my mind.

"Come on! Hurry up! I have something special planned, just for us"

My heart raced, and the adrenaline pumped around my body, I'm not sure if it was weakness or all part of the test, but I gave in. I followed her through the forest, we ran, hand in hand, young lovers without a care in the world, exactly how it used to be.

The evening sun was warm on my skin, the air, sweet and fresh like mint chocolate chip ice cream. I felt free, happy, my worries drifted away, and I felt safe. Natasha's eyes sparkled and twinkled like the stars above, her hair was longer than before, waves of her locks glistened like silk ribbons, they had a mind of their own and danced in the breeze.

She led me deeper into the forest, sounds of wildlife surrounded us, chirping squirrels raced alongside. As we flew through the forest Natasha suddenly stopped, wondering why, I glanced at her,

"Perfect" she whispered to herself.

We reached a clearing, the trees stood and towered in a perfect circle around a wooden pavilion, it stood in the middle, covered in vines and moss, it was held together by flora and fauna.

"inside?" I asked, she nodded and stepped seductively into the structure, with each step slowly placing her cute toes on the structure, swaying her hips back and forth. She placed her hands on the railing and waited. I followed behind her and wrapped my arms around her waist. Her perfume was sharp yet delicate, Orange Blossom and Spanish Jasmine, it made me want her more, a raw ache from deep within. I spun her around and kissed her passionately.

Her lips were soft, and her breath warm. She kissed me back, her tongue exploring mine, her hand stroking the back of my neck. I felt my arousal growing, and so did she. I pressed hard against her, the warmth from her body drove me insane with desire.

"I need you!" I pleaded, my heart beated fast in my chest, I was desperate for her. The pounding was unbearable and filled with anticipation, everything of the room before was gone, truly wrapped in the moment. She had me.

"What are you waiting for then," she purred, "take me!"

I lifted her effortlessly and carried her across the structure, a pile of blankets and cushions laid perfectly in the corner of the pavilion, I laid her gently down,

"Take me now, my love."

She stroked her collarbone and slowly removed her dress, the material fell naturally away from her body, revealing herself to me.

I stood, clumsily tearing off my shirt and kicking my boots away, every moment away from her felt like pain. Her skin was warm, her scent intoxicating. I stroked her cheek and brushed her hair from her face, she moaned with pleasure. I could resist her no longer, she took me in her arms, we became one.

The sensation was intense, I struggled to control myself. Her hands gripped me, and her legs wrapped tightly around my waist. She bit my lip and pulled my hair. This was something else, it didn't feel like her, didn't feel…real. Something foul was at play, I had to stop, this wasn't her.

"No! Please, no, don't do this," I yelled.

Natasha laughed a deep throaty laugh, her voice changing as she spoke,

"Come to me, let me be with you…I need you," she cried and convulsed.

I watched her body go limp, her eyes rolled into the back of her head and she stopped fighting, her warmth that was so comforting and soothing left, her body was cold to touch and the colour drained from her, the feeling of her last breath leaving haunts me even today. I looked up as I rose to my feet, afraid and horrified. Did I cause this? Was this a trick or a test? I panicked and looked around for help, a dark shadowy figure in the distance stood, motionless, staring. He locked onto me like a hunter scoping its prey. I couldn't make out who, but it looked familiar.

"Stop! End the test! End it NOW!" Sgt Ackerman's voice screamed as the surroundings dissolved, I woke up on an operating table. My arms and legs were bound to the frame.

"It's okay, you're okay. Take a few moments, calm down, it's over. Breathe. You're okay." a voice I recognised tried to reassure me. I could feel tears stinging my eyes, I had been crying and shaking.

"I killed her... She was scared, I didn't mean to hurt her. Is she okay? Is she alive?"

"Yes, she is perfectly fine. It was all an illusion, it's alright. She is okay." Sgt Ackerman reassured me.

"It was just a dream?" I asked.

"You could say that. The machine you're in scans your memories, dreams and thoughts, and creates an alternate reality in your mind. This is how we can find out the things that haunt you, or that may affect you in battle."

"What the fuck is going on?! Get me the hell out of here, right now!" I demanded. The rest of the team watched in horror, they stood on the deck above leaning over the barriers, like on-lookers at a crash site, they glared with horrific anticipation.

"Get me out! Let me go! I want out! Back off!" The test understandably had me shook, I would never do that, nor did I want to ever go through anything like it again.

My heart rate increased, I could feel it beat inside my head, the sound was deafening, the monitor next to me beeped loudly, it was getting too much, too intense. My bindings were too weak and snapped with no resistance. The electronics in the room sparked and crackled, chaos began to erupt as the light flickered and exploded, without warning there was silence, the room was pitch black. I took a deep breath, and exhaled, the outburst was too much, I passed out.

———

Melodic chirping woke my slumber, my body was drained and felt weak, heavy. The soft rustle of the breeze through the trees, and the smell of bacon and eggs cooking, further woke me and gained my full attention. I rolled over and found a tray of food.

My hands were still shaking as I lifted the silver lid covering the food, my mouth watered as I tucked in, it tasted divine, a lardon and ostrich egg rice bowl with melted provolone, the eggs were cooked to perfection, salted and slightly runny in the centre. I looked around the room and was surprised to find the bed I was in was segregated from the others, not some hospital cot, or a triple bunk, but a room to myself. How long had I been asleep for? Where was everybody else? Questions without answers.

"Morning, I trust you slept well?" The Sergeant called as she knocked and opened the door at the same time, privacy wasn't a thing in the military, you belonged to something bigger, served the country, you had no need for privacy or secrets. Sgt Ackerman had a look of sympathy with a side of guilt, I could tell that what happened previously, was a mistake, and a big one. At this point I wasn't too familiar with Ackerman, I wasn't sure if I could trust her, maybe she was just touching base trying to get a feel for the situation, trying to see if I would turn and report her for what happened, or if she genuinely cared for my well-being.

"Uh, yeah, what happened? Where are the others?" the groggy daze still had its effect on me, like a heavy cloud blocking the path between my mouth and brain.

"You had a panic attack, the restraints broke and your body went into overdrive, your vitals were through the roof!, you passed out, the others are still sleeping in the dorm, the test is a lot harder on the first day."

"You said it was a mistake, what do you mean?"

Sarge sighed, reluctant to answer "The test is supposed to be random, a simulation of a life-or-death situation, the program was hacked, it was supposed to test your decision-making instead it read your thoughts and feelings and played a sadistic game, We believe someone rigged the test"

"Why? Who would want to do that?" I was confused, I had no enemies then, a young pup.

"We don't know, but we're going to find out."

"Eat up, shower and join us in the briefing room when you're ready," the Sergeant turned and left the room, still with the straight back and military hop-skip.

I didn't know what to expect. The rest of the team were seated around a large round table, and greeted me as I took a seat. I could feel their questioning looks, wondering what the hell happened and If I was the crazy loose cannon of the team, one they needed to keep an eye on. I avoided any communication and waited patiently for the Sergeant to begin.
"Good Morning everyone, as you know, a few of our members had a difficult experience yesterday," her eyes darted in my direction. A few? We all knew it was just me, I appreciated the effort to normalise the 'problem'...even if the problem was me "This has highlighted a few areas of weakness in the system and security protocols, however, we still need to proceed with training as planned" she explained, " The Lt General wants a fully effective team

ASAP! Today is going to be a little more relaxed, we will be running some exercises, and testing your fitness levels" I still had no idea of what 'skills' I possessed, Why I was chosen or what the others could do. My only hope was that I could keep up and not stand out too much. Being the weakest in class was a new experience for me, I was usually the strongest, sometimes taking the role of mentor or teacher, but this was horrible, like wading through thick oil while everyone was dry and running laps on me.

The room was a mixture of emotions, excitement, dread, fear and uncertainty. I was a mix of all four, it was nauseating, my breakfast was fighting its way back up, I swallowed hard and forced the thick knot back down, I had to focus and not lose my composure…again.

"So, let's get started," the Sergeant smiled. Let's get started? I'd heard that before, same tone, same apprehensive pause between words. I didn't put two and two together at the time, my mind was fixed on other, more pressing issues.

"Sergeant Ackerman," I approached as the rest left the room "would it be possible to ask a few questions about the test yesterday, or perhaps discuss a few theories on why it happened?"

"I'm Listening"

"What was the test supposed to be like, and why did it change?"

"Well, that's the million-dollar question, the test is tailored to your abilities, hidden subconsciously, or it was supposed to be, A simulation designed to see how you respond under pressure, the computer analyses the results and adapts the best protocol, then we tailor your training to develop you into a better soldier."

"But the system was hacked? What happened?"

"We have no idea, it's like the system was re-written, it was a complete wipe and replaced with a different code"

"Sarge, I'd like to have another go!"

"Really, so soon?"

"if it's okay with you" I wanted to make sure they didn't give up on me, I knew I had it in me, I just didn't know what 'It' was. My grandiose sense of purpose refused to let them tag me as a lost cause, the MMA, one step at a time, keep moving forward mentality took point.

"Ok, let me allocate an observation room and we'll have another stab…hour tops, you're sure you're ok to do this?"

"Yeah, I think I'm ready," I smiled, hiding my uncertainty.

"Alright, I'll have everything set up, but you have to promise me, if it gets too much, you quit, no arguments"

"Ok, thanks Sarge,"

I spent the next hour contemplating the possible outcomes. Why did I want to try again, what did I hope to prove, what was the point? I felt like I had to redeem myself, show everyone I was stronger. I needed answers, answers to why I was chosen for this team. Why did I get a letter straight from the Lt General requesting me?

"Right, we've set you up in a different room, rule out any possibilities for another disaster" Sarge reached into her left breast pocket and pulled out a small metallic pill, dull black with speckles of silver swirling in a sporadic motion.

"Down the hatch!" She offered me some water and smiled.

"What? No scary guy with welder goggles?" I was confused, why go through all the horror antics if I could just take a pill.

Sarge laughed "That's for first timers, you already know where you're going, a meeting with the Acerbic Bicuspid would be pointless" the name certainly matched the creature, Acerbic Bicuspid. The world beyond Saint Morgan was strange and dark. I swallowed the pill, took a mouthful of water and washed it around my mouth before swallowing with a big gulp.

"What now?" I was a little more apprehensive this time, knowing where I was going and what could happen.

"Just lay back, make yourself comfortable" I swung my legs back on the bed and fidgeted into a perfect position.

The room slowly went dark and my senses dulled, my eyes heavily drifted into slumber.

I woke up in the same pavilion, this time I was alone, to my relief Natasha wasn't there. The pillows and blankets hugged my body as I lay in anticipation, I wasn't sure what to do, I stood up slowly and looked for the mysterious figure, no luck either.

The pavilion stood in a clearing, perfectly central, surrounded by a field of headstones. I was in a cemetery, the realisation shook me, tingles shivered down my neck, what was I doing in a cemetery.

The Fall of Saint Morgan

Days of old, Memories of gold

Gone are the days of innocence,
Replaced by acts of malevolence.
Once a place of comfort and peace,
Now shattered by unrest and disease.

Gone are the days of solace and calm,
Replaced by shadows of harm,
What once was a sanctuary, now a war zone,
Leaving us feeling lost and alone.

We must fight to reclaim our sacred space,
To restore love and trust in this place,
For we cannot let fear win the day,
Our safe haven will rise again, come what may.

The sun blazed its hot rays on the pitch black tar, the roads emitted waves of heat and danced as they escaped to the sky. Temperatures soared on that Tuesday, it reached a blistering Forty-Two degrees celcius, and it was getting hotter every minute that passed. The air was humid, making the temperature seem even higher. People were running around on the streets, trying to escape the heat by entering into shops and bars. Searching for shade, or something that would keep them cool.

Saint Morgan in late July always experienced hot summers, but this was particularly unbearable. The record of the highest temperature was broken a week ago, and it had no sign of relenting.

People sat in the shadows, hiding from the merciless heat and hoping for a sudden downpour. The heat was so bad, that the police were driving around handing care packages of water and fruit to passers by.

A young boy, no older than ten, came hurtling out of Geraldine's corner shop. Running home with a few groceries in hand, his mama promised him spaghetti meatballs for dinner and cookie dough ice cream for dessert, a promise like that could not be passed. With the plastic bag swinging in his hand, He had to make sure that nothing would fall out, a double knot held his dinner secure. His shirt clung to his sweaty skin, his breath heavily panting, rhythmically to the pounding of his steps, he made his way through the sweltering heat, darting past people and around corners.

The boy ran in pure excitement, his legs were screaming in pain, and the plastic bag was heavy in his grip. He was just two houses away from his home, a raised concrete tile protruding from the level pavement stuck out, the corner stood up a good few inches, The boy lost his footing and stumbled forward landing on his hands and knees. The blood seeped from his grazes and stung painfully.

"That wasn't there before..." The boy muttered under his breath between gasps of pain as he rubbed his saw knee.

He slowly stood up and grabbed the plastic bag which had fallen from his grip. He was about to open the front door to his house, but was stopped by a voice behind him.

"Benjamin!" a gruff voice boomed.

The boy turned around and was met with the sight of nothing, just the street and the sun beating down. He turned back to the front door.

"BENJAMIN!" The same gruff voice screamed, a towering shadow crept over him.

The boy turned his head back, seeing a giant figure standing behind him, staring down at him. The boy's eyes opened, fear had become him, his jaw dropped. The towering figure was as black as coal, Black like the absence of light. Black as the night, the colour of his soul. The darkness that the sun could not penetrate.

"Are you going to answer me?" the figure bellowed.

The boy stood still, unmoving, frozen under a spell. The only sign that the boy was alive was his blinking eyes and the rise and fall of his chest as he breathed heavily.

"Wh...who, who. Im" the boy stuttered, barely a whisper. "MAMA!!" The boy gathered all his strength and called out for help

"Feeble being!" the figure muttered, scoffing at the boy. Disappointed by the boy's response he engulfed him in shadow, wisps of smoke coiled and embraced his body. Cracking of bones and snapping of joints filled the air. The boy's screams were sickening like a pig being slaughtered. His flesh, stretched and pulled. His clothes tore off of his body, the only thing that remained were the tatters and pieces of fabric.

"AHHHHH!!!"

His bones snapped and bent into awkward positions. His eyes bulged, blood dripped from his tear ducts. His mouth opened in a silent scream. The figure released the boy, and the boy fell to the floor in a heap, lifeless.

"Rise! My minion...Rise" The shadow spoke, with a strong commanding tone

Limbs snapped as the figure rose to stand, crooked and bent, disfigured in a pile of dripping flesh. It did not answer, it did not have a voice, nor mouth, nor face

"Follow" the figure said as he disappeared into a dark alley, the creature followed, shambling along, leaving a trail of blood behind as it wobbled from left to right, it looked back and grinned. The terrifying darkness had devoured the town and twisted the bodies of everyone caught in it; Pazandir's army had reached Saint Morgan.

"Natasha honey, come help me set the table," Lily called out from the kitchen, Natasha was in her room writing letters to Sebastian, she spent a lot of time making sure each letter was perfectly handwritten and each letter curled with beautiful calligraphy. It was around half four in the afternoon and William was due any minute, a long shift on duty made him especially hungry.

"Coming ma" She licked the last envelope and pressed it tight, sealing the glue. The front door opened with a click and a loud thud as William fumbled the keyhole and shoved the door with his shoulder. He grunted as he closed the door behind him.

"Honey, is that you?" Lily called out

"Yeah," he said with a heavy sigh.

"Dinner is almost ready, I just need some help setting the table"

"Be right there"

Lily smiled to herself, happy that her husband was finally home, the sound of footsteps approached her, and she turned around. Lily was met with the sight of William in his work uniform, his navy blue shirt and black slacks were still in pristine condition, William took great care over his appearance.

"Welcome home" she said as she kissed him on the lips, and she turned back around to continue chopping the vegetables.

"Thank you, how was your day?" William said as he hugged her from behind and gently kissed her neck.

"It was fine, but I do think the weather is getting worse," Lily replied. "It's so hot" She fanned herself, Sweat gathered on her forehead, the tiny fan on the kitchen windowsill spun like crazy trying to cool the room.

"Well it's the summer, I'm not surprised" William chuckled

"Well, the summers are normally not this bad," Lily said. "How was your day?" she asked, wanting to change the topic.

"Oh, my day was boring, there was not a lot to do, the town is peaceful" William said.

"That's good to hear, peaceful is good " Lily said, relieved, she hated the idea of William going out and potentially risking his life.

William let go, and headed upstairs to change, passing Natasha on the stairs. "Go set the table, I'll be down any sec" He said.

"Ok" Natasha answered.

She entered the dining room and laid out three plates, each having a knife and fork by the side. She placed a bowl at the centre of the table and placed a jug of water next to it. Just as she was finished, the doorbell rang, Lily walked in with the food and set it on the table.

"Who can that be?" She said as she turned around and went to answer the door.

The Sun began to fade, like clouds filled with rain, slowly drifting along. A cool uncomfortable breeze drifted through the air. The wind danced through the trees and leaves, making an erratic rustling sound.

As Lily approached the door, it flung open knocking her backwards. She gasped in pain, clutching her face, a gash appeared across her left eye. Blood seeped from her wound.

"What the f- " William ran down the stairs, his gun poised at the front door above Lily, he stood in front of her shielding her from harm. "Who's there?!" He yelled

"MORETTI!" a deep voice boomed.

William stood there frozen in shock, his gun shook in his hands, the shadowed figure had made its way through the town and had arrived at the Miller's family home. William's heart pounded against his ribcage, his pulse was racing, he felt his muscles tense, the sweat trickled down his back.

"Don't move!" he called out.

"Mmm Someone with clout!" the dark figure was impressed, its shadowy tentacle reached out.

"Police! Freeze!" William fired his handgun twice, aiming dead central and bang on target.

Black wisps curled around the bullet mixing with the crisp air, for a second William could see through, past the figure, onto the drive outside. The dark figure formed back and demanded "MORETTI!"

William's face dropped, his eyes widening. The shadow stood toe to toe with William and paused, William was defenceless, he stood, gazing into the darkness "Natasha! RUN!" William shouted, his face painted white in fear, his voice cracked.

"Dad?" Natasha said, as she entered the room, a loud snap and a crack was heard, Lily gasped, she looked at her husband and then back to her daughter. "No, Nn...no" Lily screamed in agony.

William's body hung limply in the air, his body twisted, his neck snapped. Natasha stood there frozen, her face full of terror. Lily's heart sank, she couldn't move, tears rolled down her cheeks, her eyes were bloodshot.

"No, no, no, no. NO!" Lily sobbed

"Run Natasha" She cried, her face drenched with tears. "Please run!"

Natasha was terrified, her breathing became erratic.

"RUN!"

Her heart, pounding, her chest felt tight. She couldn't move, her feet were planted firmly to the ground.

The dark figure loomed over Lily, casting her in shadow, black wisps curled around her throat and tightened. She clawed at her throat, trying to breathe, her lungs, burning, her body convulsed. Her mouth agape, gasping for air, the world grew dark. The last thing she saw was her husband, and the last thing she heard was Natasha's scream.

"MAAAA!"

She couldn't breathe, her hands dropped limply to her side, and her body fell to the floor.

Natasha bolted towards the kitchen, grabbing a knife, and her phone, she ran upstairs to her room, slamming the door shut and locking it. She ran to the far corner and dialled 911, her fingers trembling. The monotone beep on the phone echoed through the room.

"Come on, come on, pick up" she muttered to herself, her eyes darting across the room.

She could hear the apparition from downstairs, it crept around the ground floor, she could feel the house shaking. A sudden crash and a boom came from below her, and she knew that her mama and pops was gone. Grunting and heavy breathing came from her father, he was moving, he was walking around the house.

"Come on, come on, pick up, pick up, pick up!" She cried, she was panicking, her mind was racing, her thoughts were chaotic.

She could hear the thing dragging her mother and father around the house, like puppets to its master.

"NATASHA!" It called out.

It was close, the floorboards creaked and moaned, it was in her parent's bedroom. She could hear the thing sniffing around, looking for her, searching the house. It reached her room.

"NATASHA!"

The door handle twisted and shook violently. before the door flung open

"NATASHA!" it screamed, a guttural scream.

Her heart was pounding, her breath was ragged, tears poured down her cheeks. The shadow paused, it did not take her, it just stood there, waiting. It had other plans for her.

"Hello? This is 911, how can I help" the voice on the phone was calm and collected.

Natasha dropped her phone, the demonic being, an amalgamation of her mother and father entered the room, its jaw wide open and its hands clawed, blood dripped as it slowly advanced towards Natasha. It gathered up its intestines like a rope and bound her hands and feet, the wet squelching against her hands made her gag, the thought of her parents being manipulated, their organs used as binds, her body defenceless but still able to experience the horror. Natasha screamed, she kicked and struggled but she was trapped.

The shadowed figure dispersed from the house together with the horrific beings, leaving the house empty.

Necromancy

Talking to the dead

In twilight's hush, where shadows dance and play,
I stumbled upon a forbidden way,
A dark art long forgotten, lost in time,
Necromancy, the whispered rhyme.

With each new discovery, my heart did race,
As I learned to summon spirits to the place,
To bend to my will, to do my bidding,
And grant me power, beyond my wildest
thinking.

But beware, dear seeker, of the price to pay,
For necromancy, a path that's hard to stay,
Can lead to madness, and a soul's decay,
And leave you lost, in a world of disarray.

The pavilion stood in a clearing, perfectly central, surrounded by a field of headstones. I was in a cemetery? The realisation shook me, tingles shivered down my neck, what was I doing in a cemetery.

My breath quickened as my heart started to race, I felt like an intruder, someone was going to leap out of the darkness and attack me, at least, that's what I kept telling myself.

"Pull yourself together Seb, you got this" I muttered under my breath, desperately trying to muster the courage to venture further.

I crept around the pavilion towards the steps, out into the cemetery, darting my head around trying to make sense of the situation. Slowly I advanced to the steps, taking each movement with care, I couldn't fail again, I needed to make a good impression.

The area was built in circles with the pavilion in the centre expanding out like an archery target, headstones and fresh graves lay in sporadic placements, probably to squeeze in the most bodies. The Smell of pine had a rotten taint, like a musty mothball or raw chicken that had slightly turned, it added to my unease and made me queasy. Darting left and right strategically, weaving in and out of the stones I tried to not disturb the dead, each step I took the ground moaned in painful despair. The moaning grew louder and louder,

"Uurrrrr, stride left, aim west" The voices beneath started to make sense, they guided me. I followed.

I couldn't shake the image of the open graves, bodies laying half animated, their heads following my every movement, their mouths open in silent screams, eyes wide and unblinking.

"Stop, right, turn 45 degrees" I complied, my breathing was heavy, the uncertainty and horror began to take hold. "Uuurrr, 10 steps ahead, you will see it" I stepped forward and there it was, a small, white headstone with a small candle and a rose, the words were blurred, worn away by time and weather. I walked closer, intrigued as to why this headstone was significant, why I was guided here.

Clumping my sleeve into a ball in my hand I scrubbed the letter to reveal the words,

'Lily & William Miller'

The shock and horror caused me to stumble backwards, I couldn't stop shaking and the tears were uncontrollable, "How?" My heart sank as I collapsed on the ground, the earth shook and crumbled. The simulation ended.

The feeling of power rushed through my veins, imbuing me with gifts, the anxiety flushed out of my body like a flood down a drain. It was as if all of the fear and stress, the anger and sorrow were replaced with a warm and comfortable throb, a sense of belonging washed over me, finally.

The harrowing events in the test were just that right? A simulation fabricated to test my will, to push me to the edge. It unlocked something inside, It wasn't…real? I was left with more questions than answers. Who were the dead and why did they help me, it was like solving a puzzle without all the pieces. The last image of Lily &

William Miller on the gravestone kept running through my mind, was it real?

Days had passed like a flash, maybe my mind was focused elsewhere, maybe training kept me busy, grunt work will do that, It has a way of occupying the brain just enough so you don't focus on the real things.

—

Sgt Ackerman barged through the door, early as usual, what she found made her take a step back, threw her off guard for a sec. "Good morning Sarge!" As I pretended to check my watch, knowing full well we both knew the time "Not quite early enough" I flicked the frying pan tossing the eggs and sausages, whilst shuffling the smaller pan on my left, both burners on high heat with a roaring flame, cracking bacon sizzled in a pool of oil and fat. "I've made plenty if you want some, it's just going on a plate now. The others are ready and waiting" We both looked over at the metal canteen-style table behind me, the horde of ravaged beasts banging fork and knife gathered, glared impatiently. The Pop of the toaster interrupted the grotesque show and our eyes locked back on each other. Sarge didn't answer, I didn't expect her to, she frowned her mouth and nodded as if to say 'I'm impressed, carry on'. She stood at the door for a few minutes, watching, before turning to close it behind her, "An extra 15 min soldiers, enjoy" she didn't shout but the message was delivered and received, the room exploded in a flurry of cheers and chanting. I served up a plate, adding a couple of slices of bacon to the heap of salty grease and fat. It was if the team had accepted me, made me one of them, as soon as they knew I wasn't an average joe they had all become very protective of me, a brotherhood of sorts, I wasn't the first, nor would I be the last, they would give their life for each other and now for me. We ate like animals, hunger got the better of us, the truth was we ate very well everyday, but training took its toll, drills, exercise, ability training, it was relentless but necessary. I'd been at the camp for five weeks now, the harrowing scenes of my girlfriend and her parents gravestones started to fade into memories, afterall, it was just a test. A simulation.

We all lined up and headed out to meet with Sgt Ackerman, it was a nice day, the sun shone brightly, I looked at my watch, 0513. Perfect!

"Good morning Sergeant!" My confidence over time rose and I became comfortable with the chain of command.

"Morning team!, you're early, breakfast was good I hope," The Team nodded to each other, rubbing their bellies, belching and chewing the last remains.

"Team Drills, military formations and combining skills to overcome obstacles" Sarge reeled off the order of the day, then she looked at me and grinned, "Moretti! Necromancy training and leadership skills" The team lacked a leader amongst the group and needed someone to step up, I think Sarge wanted a volunteer, she opted to delegate the responsibility to me. I was a little confused, I had never experienced any kind of leadership role. I stepped forward and followed Sarge to a clearing in the forest, "You are an asset to the team, your skills will help you be not only a great addition but a great leader, your ability to fight is impressive, but, as with everything there are things you can learn, this is not an order, but advice, choose to be the leader they need. Follow your instincts, use Necromancy" Sarge walked off, I was on my own, the sun was higher now, I felt its warmth, the air was fresh and clean. I could hear birds chirping away and the sound of the guys running drills in the distance. I closed my eyes and took a deep breath, filling my lungs deeply and sharply emptying them. Over and over, I lowered my heart rate and entered a meditative state, my arms raised to a horizontal position, this opened my chest further. My surroundings darkened, the smell of pine weakend and the birds fell silent. I could feel the cold creep over me, it wasn't unpleasant now, but a familiar feeling that promised hope. I opened my eyes.

It was night, the forest was alive with sounds, crickets scraped against their wings, over and over, the croak echoed through the space, the wind whipped the treetops whistling through the branches. Stars beamed rays of light in all directions illuminating the area.

"Nǐ hǎo, young Moretti" an old, raspy voice croaked before clearing his throat,

"You can see me, can't you?" I looked around eager to put a face to the voice, but I couldn't see anything

"Indeed" the clearing of his throat did nothing, his voice was still broken and caked in phlegm, years of strong liquor had loosened his vocal cords, lengthening his base tones.

"This is different, it's a pleasure to…meet you?" Questions raced through my mind as this stranger entered my mind, I couldn't see him or recognise his voice,

"My name is Yìchén, I am an old Samurai master, nobody else can see or hear me, Nobody can hear you talking to me either." I nodded, trying to keep my cool. Instructions from an actual Samurai flooded my mind and freaked me out.

"Sgt Ackerman needs us to bond, I need you to learn the potential of what we can do together"

"How can you help me?"

"I can see your world, be your eyes and ears. While you're in mine, time stands still."

I was amazed, a skilled warrior giving me guidance in the field was just like coach Adkins shouting instructions onside of the octagon.

"Are you ready to try something?"

"Yes" I smiled, curious and pumped, excited for a challenge.

The world transformed, swirls of reds and greens engulfed us both as we teleported. The patchy, green grass beneath my feet disappeared, cold grey tiles click-clacked in place and built a high rise building around us. I sat in an open space, dark grey tiles ran from floor to ceiling, a row of cashier desks lined the far wall. Soft plush seats sat around a round table in front of me. The distant sound of voices chatting and the hum of the air conditioning unit, completed the simulation.

"What is this place?" I asked

"Training simulation, I will spot vital information, if you make it to the roof, we're ready"

I stood carefully, and looked around. The jarring tintinnabulation started the simulation, like the bell at school indicating the day's end. Crowds flooded and filled the room, all in office attire, a mob of men and women. Going about their business like I wasn't there, I preferred it that way. I walked slowly, not to draw attention, keeping my head down, soaking up everything I could. Yichén fed information as It came to him, keeping us alive.

"6ft male, office blue shirt with a dark purple tie, 3 o'clock, crew cut, reaching for the gun on his belt"

I glanced at 3, his eyes gazed at me like a predator at its prey, it felt like the room honed in on just the two of us.

I took a slight detour, moving slightly through the crowd, keeping composure, circling around for a closer position, I managed to lose his gaze and gain a closer stance. I grabbed his arm and twisted hard, the gun fell as I caught it with my left hand. The cold steel felt comfortable and weighted. I raised the weapon, two in the chest, one in the head. His body transformed into green blocks and tumbled onto the floor, he disappeared.

"Good job!"

The rabble of the simulated crowd ignored the gunfire and continued their business, so did I. I moved slowly, giving Yichén a chance.

"Look! Sign on the elevator! 'Out of order' Stairs, take the stairs on your left"

A single grey door appeared, *'click'* is if the simulation was on my side the door unlocked, I reached for the handle and entered a narrow stairway. Cream painted concrete walls spiralled for what seemed like forever, the warmth from the heaters didn't reach this part of the building, the chill was a surprising comfort, considering the circumstance, a bead of sweet dried before it could run down my cheek. I ascended floor by floor, pistol in hand and pointed ahead.

"Take the exit onto the fourth floor, they're coming down the stairs!"

Yichén guided me perfectly, I could hear the charge of henchmen barreling down above me, in one fell motion, I grabbed the handle and rammed the door with my shoulder, the glare from the large office windows blinded me for a second, catching me off guard. I shook my head and adjusted my eyes to the light,

"Moretti!" Yichén yelled desperately gaining my attention

A large figure cracked his knuckles and darted right, out of sight.

My youth and stupidity got the better of me, I sprinted towards him, ignoring Yichén's guide.

"Seb! Watch out from behind the separation wall, on your Right!"

A woman appeared, exactly where Yichén said. She launched with a sprouting roundhouse, knocking me down, square on the jaw too. Disorientated and dazed I fumbled around on my knees, she got me good and proper.

"Josei-Ki Sebastian, we gotta work together, listen to me!"

Yichén's voice was muffled and echoed as I blinked, gathering my surroundings. I stood tall and took a deep breath, holding my hands in a Philly-shell guard, my left hand at my stomach, my right under my chin.

The woman came charging towards me, the sound of her footsteps were heavy in steel toe cap boots, she was a large individual, Not fat but built like a bodybuilder, dressed in tactical combat gear, she wore 8 oz fingerless gloves too. I ducked under her punch, her fist connected with the drywall behind me. As she tried to retrieve her hand from the wall, I swung with a right at her temple. The blow connected, staggering her backwards, allowing me to launch my knee upwards to her chin.

She crumpled to the floor, out cold. Green dust faded and disappeared into the floor.

I took a deep breath and let it out slowly. I had to stay focused. "Sorry Yichén"

I turned and darted off, down the corridor to the end, I turned right and saw the sign on the glass double doors. It wasn't like the other signs, this one didn't fit in. The neon words flashed, on the left 'going up' in blue and on the right 'follow him' in red.

"Yichén?" I stood totally bewildered by the choice ahead.

Nothing, I got Nothing. Yichén ignored me. I knew we had to progress to the roof.

"I'll be fine, Yichén, I know I can take him!"

"No Sebastian, you need to listen to me, I've been with you through all of this, I'm here to help and protect us!"

The thunderous stampede of guards got louder and louder, I had to make a choice and quickly.

"Fuck! Fuck sake! Fuck! Alright!"

I opened the glass door, the elevator at the end of the hallway was large, built to carry large cargo. The doors opened, the mirror reflected a beat-up, worn down sorry mother fucker, took me a second glance to realise, it was me.

"Damn!" I held my chin and turned left to right, examining the damage.

I turned round to face the doors, not sure if it was out of disgust at my reflection or the preparation of what was waiting for me. The low hum-drum of the elevator motor churned, but not for long.

'bing'

The doors opened to a nightclub, flashes of vivid red and royal blues flooded the room, wisps of smoke crept over the dancefloor, the shimmer of the glass bottles against the mirror backdrop ran across the room's perimeter behind the bar. The dance floor was empty and the DJ booth unmanned.

I stepped out onto the hardwood floor, the thud of my feet, amplified by the lack of life. A slow bass guitar played a simple riff, over and over the tune thumped and bounced around the empty room, the volume rolled to high, methodic, like a heartbeat. I left my gun on the office floor, I had to resort to hand to hand combat, pretty hard with multiple targets.

"You're a hard man to kill" a voice erupted from the shadows.

"He rallied troops, with strength and might, to stand against the tyrant's sight, with courage bold and heart unbroken, they marched to war, their banners unspoken."

The singer's deep, expressive contralto vocals and raspy tone moaned expressions as the final fight emerged, Men and women dressed in monochrome suits swallowed up the dancefloor, pouring from both sides of the room.

They circled each other waiting for me to descend to their level, I slowly took each step darting my eyes back and forth keeping track of every enemy.

"I'll call them out, we can do this!" Yichén was confident, I wasn't.

I played with my shirt cufflinks, tugging my sleeve tight, rolling my left shoulder, easing the stiffness of swelling. I clicked my neck left to right.

The band changed octave, and the pace quickened.

"In the face of fear, they stood tall, And marched into the fray, Never backing down or turning back, No matter the price to pay,"

The first opponent attacked. Yichén stepped in and alerted me before he could strike.

"Right side! Uppercut, left hook!"

I continued to the centre of the dancefloor, surrounded in a perfect circle. I danced, dodging attacks from left and right as the band's tempo raced to match the pace. Flying knees and haymakers were useless against Yichén and I, we worked perfectly in sync, we were one.

"Behind! Duck, spinning hook, uppercut to the chin!"

The dance continued, as the battle raged.

"Three more to go! One behind the DJ booth, duck right!"

I dove towards the ground, rolling forward, over my shoulder, a single shot rang out, the bullet ricochet off the hard wooden flooring, just inches away.

"Now, Moretti!"

I rose to my feet and charged forward, spinning my right leg and letting the kinetic force fly, my body glided through the air. The single blow connected with his ribs, the crack echoed through the room, louder than the band, he crumpled to the floor in pain. The final two approached at the same time, one on the left, the other on the right.

"White Polo shirt on the left! Right hook to ribs, He'll swing and crack your chin so duck low and aim for his neck with your left on your way up"

I thought I was untouchable with Yichén, I was wrong. The other didn't take the time to wait and Yichén didn't catch everything.

His jumping spinning kick found its target, the lower portion of my back. I fell to my knees, the wind knocked out of me. I looked over my shoulder.

"Shit! Sorry Seb!" The pain in Yichén's voice made it clear, it affected him too.

The henchman stood smug and waited for my retort. The arrogance poured as he glared through his eyebrows, tilting his head down, grinning with one side of his mouth.

"On your feet! He'll try that kick again, catch it! Sweep his leg and follow with a ground and pound!" Yichén sounded more and more like Coach Adkins.

I mounted him in a dominant position, his face was a delight, he didn't expect a thing. I continued with vicious elbows, over and over till his broken, bloodied face fazed out.

The room emptied and the simulation was over. It took me a while to calm down, the rush of the fight had my adrenaline at peak. I stared at Sarge with eyes wide, unsure of who she was. I could tell it took her back, for a second or two she was intimidated by me, she saw the demon within.

Deliverance of Woe

Out of the fire

With sword in hand and shield held high
You must vanquish evil, do not shy
For the people look to you
To protect them, see them through

Through peril and strife, you must prevail
Your courage and strength shall never fail
A hero born, a champion true
For the greater good, all you must do

The world shakes beneath my feet
As I struggle to find my seat
In this storm of sorrow and pain
Where nothing will ever be the same

Training had continued like clockwork, up at the crack of dawn and back in the simulation. Things were going smoothly, I was making fantastic progress, it just wasn't fast enough, don't get me wrong, my team supported me and congratulated me every step of the way. I was impatient and eager to push myself. Sessions with Yichén were getting longer and stronger. We began to know each other, we formed a mutual respect, a bond, similar to a father and son, a master and his student. The Team bonded well too, within a couple of months we found ourselves spending every minute together, bunking in the same room, eating the same meals at the same time. The only time we had alone was the time spent training our individual abilities.

I truly established my position as team leader, the guys voted for me, a unanimous decision, with the help of Sarge poking me in the right direction. The team showed trust in my abilities. Running drills over and over, like a broken record, but that's what needed to happen, our team needed to be on peak performance, we were already considered the best of the best in the eyes of the military, but in our eyes, there was always room for improvement.

Friday nights came quickly, pizza and beers, a treat for the hard work over the week. The guys were chilling out, playing video games and shooting pool. Tunes on the antique jukebox played classic rock, BloodPool and AcidRain were fantastic soundtracks for video games and beer. I sat at the bar, watching my team, I sipped on Ice cold beer, the hoppy suds refreshed my mouth with each swig, the heavy pizza left me with a bloated gut. The lemon wedge provided a sharp twist that hit the spot everytime. Time away from training felt nice, we were too young to waste our time worrying constantly about a war we had no part in, not yet anyway, the conflict between the three factions had not fully developed, whispers of little spats and bar brawls filled the rumormill. This piqued our interest, we were trained with weapons, ready for what we thought was war, we had no idea of the reality that would hit us.

"Hey, Moretti, come shoot some pool with us," Jameson called over to me, holding both pool cues in one hand.

"Hell yeah!" I replied, I loved playing pool.

The game was fun, competitive, just like training. Jameson and Em were on one team, Church waved me over and high fived me, She opened up over the weeks, took her time but eventually we formed a friendship, I knew it was her past haunting her that kept her quiet, something she had gone through, but I never asked, I wasn't going to force her. When she was ready she'd tell me everything she wanted to.

"Moretti, you and Church, You're goin' down" As Jameson broke, the pool balls flew and spread across the table. Sarge burst into the dorm and diverted our attention to the news, changing the TV channel.

'We interrupt your regularly scheduled programming to bring you this important message' I looked over to Church and Jameson, they had a bewildered expression of confusion and horror, the anticipation was unnerving, I'd never seen Sarge like this, rattled and on edge.

"This is Captain Dillon. I'm coming to you from a secure location. A new threat has appeared on the eastern seaboard. Shadows, disfigured bodies of limbs, Unnatual beings sweeping over towns and cities, our latest reports show Saint Morgan in ruin, the citizens slaughtered, mass genocide of the human race. The local police are no match for these creatures, they cannot be stopped, not by standard military weapons. Some lucky ones have escaped and have fled north, towards the mountains. We must act and defend ourselves, as a country, as a united front against the darkness."

"Jesus Christ." Jameson's eyes widened, he was speechless.

Church stood and walked over to the TV, her eyes fixated on the screen, "What are they?" she questioned, not taking her eyes off the screen.

"It's unclear what they are, but the government is calling them beasts of shadow. Their origin is unknown, the first report came from the east coast, but we cannot rule out a possibility of invasion, these things may be worldwide. They move in packs, tearing through any who stand in their way." Sarge had a printed report from Fort Gamboge, information and orders straight from the top.

"What the fuck..." Church's face contorted, the fear evident, her voice trembling, I'd never seen her this scared before, "I want to be with my family."

"You're here for a reason, the best of the best, Sector C Special Operations, you have been chosen to fight. These beasts, whatever they are, cannot be reasoned with, they do not listen, they are not human. They are pure evil." Sarge's words were final, she meant every word.

"Sarge, where are the others?" I asked.

"They are in briefing room 4B, preparing." Sarge was firm, I nodded and stood up, "Get yourself ready and get over there."

We all headed to the locker rooms and suited up. Our uniforms were tactical, we all had a different style but the colours and the equipment was the same, green and black, we wore Kevlar vests and armoured shoulder plates. Standard issue handguns were an aid to our abilities. We were to meet in briefing room 4B to get details of the mission. To take the fight to the beasts.

"I can't believe this is real." Jameson paced back and forth, "We are going to be fighting those things."

"Jameson, Relax." I reassured him, "This is what we've trained for."

"But this is not just a sim, this is real." He stopped pacing, his hands resting on his head. The sweat poured from his forehead, his nerves were on edge.

"Hey." Church walked in, she was ready, "I've spoken with Sarge, she said we should head over to the briefing room."

We followed her through the compound, we passed a few of the other groups, Fort Zaffre was large and we'd never seen these people before, I assumed it was just us. Soldiers looking just like us in similar uniforms with different colours indicating teams.

"I'm sure we'll get used to seeing these faces more often, Moretti." Church had a feeling, I couldn't explain it, it was as if she could read my thoughts, I nodded and smiled, putting it down to our time in close proximity.

As we entered the briefing room, all eyes were on us, the silence was deafening, all the soldiers were waiting, seated and listening to their commanding officer, who was at the front, on the stage. He paused to wait for us to be seated, the large hall echoed our footsteps, tall wooden cladding panels ran from floor to ceiling and all the way around the room, hard plastic chairs sat in rows, tight and perfectly aligned facing the stage. That's where he stood. Major Mikolasch's presence was commanding, at Seven feet and nine inches he towered over everyone, he had no reason for an elevated stage. His shoulders were square and broad, at right angles they protruded from his bulging neck, a hulking goliath. Major wore his military uniform everywhere, a short sleeve button up tucked into baggy combat trousers and laced tight into shiny black boots, Major was old school, and lived the title.

"Thank you for joining us. You've all seen Captain Dillon's message on the news, these beasts have attacked Saint Morgan and are moving south. We have little intel on the enemy but no idea where they came from. All we know is that they are a danger to humanity and standard military weapons won't work. I'm appointing Sector C Specials for recon and report, head over to Saint Morgan, find out what you can. The rest of you will spread out working from the attack site, do a general sweep of the area and scope for any abnormalities. Remember we may have civilian casualties so aid when and where you can. Report for further details to your respective sergeants. Good luck."

As Major left, the room filled with murmuring, people stood and conversed with their teammates, the sound grew louder and louder, our team was silent, we knew we'd be in the thick of it, sending the most green soldiers to recon the epicentre of the attack was a risky move, we were trained but we were not experienced.

"Sector C, you're with me," Sarge ordered. We all rose from our seats and followed her out like lost lemmings, the shock of it all had us stunned, she had a look of concern on her face. We knew her long enough to tell she was worried about us. "I know this is your first time on a real mission, this is real, this is the big league, these are not simulations, this is war."

"We'll be fine, Sarge." I said, trying to ease her worries, "We've got each other's backs."

"You'll need all the help you can get, Moretti. Your powers will only get you so far. You'll be on the frontline. I'm sending a drone ahead, the flight will take fifteen minutes, I will be your guide on your headsets, so take this time to get ready." Sarge pulled out four earpiece radios from a small box, they were lightweight, the small mic was connected to the earpiece by a small cord, it was comfortable, discrete. "I know it's scary, I remember the first time I had a real life mission. The fear you feel, that knot in your stomach, you have to learn to control that, harness it. Fear is your ally."

"I think I'm gonna be sick." Jameson was hunched over, the tension was building, his nerves were shot, "I don't want to die."

The customised Humvees rolled in, the roar and pop of the engines shook the ground, the blacked out vehicles were heavily armoured, reinforced with bullet proof glass and the metal sheet plating was strong, the tires were reinforced and had an extra layer of rubber to increase the grip, designed to be more stable on any terrain, the suspension was also improved, a heavy vehicle needed a good shock system. The smell of petrol filled the air, like burnt sugar and alcohol, the benzene evaporated in our nostrils as the engines turned off.

"This will be your ride. It's time." Sarge was stoic and unflinching, the tone she used was harsh, not her usual caring self, the time had come for us to deploy, this was not training, the weight of what was about to happen hit us, it was real.

The humvee driver stepped out "Sector C Spec Ops! Saint Morgan recon. "The rush of the base was overwhelming, the smell of diesel filled my lungs, strong gales blew my hair, the heat was blistering, it was just past midday and the sun still bore down on us. I hopped into the back, Church and Jameson followed suit with Em in front, the door closed and the hummer rumbled. The engine revved and we were on our way.

"Sector C, can you hear me?" Sarge's voice rang in our ears, her tone was firm, "I've got the drone overhead. Keep heading straight until you see the sign for Saint Morgan, turn right at the traffic lights, keep going for 2 miles. You'll see the town."

The drive was uneventful, the roads were empty, no civilians, no military, no nothing, it was quiet, a few abandoned cars and litter was scattered across the highway. No sign of life. We pulled up to the traffic lights, the intersection was empty too, the town was desolate, no movement, no sign of life, a ghost town. The Humvee pulled up and we jumped out, Memories of Saint Morgan came flooding back, the streets were familiar, after all I did grow up in Saint Morgan, but something was...off.

"What is that smell?" I gagged, the smell was a combination of blood and sulphur, pungent and foul, a putrid scent that invaded my nostrils. Gagging for breath I took a minute to regain my composure.

"Jesus Christ. What the hell happened here." Church's eyes scanned the road, looking for any signs of life.

"I think they are all dead, Church." Piles of flesh and skin scattered the roads, sporadically heaped together, the blood covered the ground and the walls, it was like a horror movie. The air was thick and clammy, the chalky dust made it hard to take a breath without choking.

"This is awful." Jameson's face was white, he couldn't believe the horror that was laid out before him.

"Let's see if we can find anyone." Church's tone was confident, she had a duty of care and was focused, I admired that, she was a strong woman.

We wandered the town, the carnage was immense, piles of human bodies were everywhere, limbs and innards spewed. This was a peaceful town, people were friendly and helpful. Saint Morgan was a place where the whole community was tight knit, the church had weekly prayer sessions, the children were educated at the local elementary and the adults worked to pay the bills, they were good people. We passed Saint Morgan's Bakery, the smell of honey and toasted oats had long gone. The sweet aroma was replaced by a metallic stench, blood and viscera painted the walls. Amelia and her husband, Peter, ran the bakery; it had been in her family for generations. Peter's uncle was a war vet, he came back to his family after being in the military, a decorated soldier. Generations of history...all gone.

"Moretti, You good?" Em noticed the sombre expression on my face. A lifetime of memories and relationships gone, replaced with horror and despair, why Saint Morgan? The most innocent kindhearted place.

"Yeah, just memories." I wiped away the tear that rolled down my cheek, "I grew up here."

"I'm sorry. I can't even imagine what you are going through." She put her hand on my shoulder and smiled, "Let's keep going, maybe we can find survivors."

We carried on, passing the bakery, the town hall and the library. The town was once the pride of the region, but now, the buildings were dilapidated, broken windows, the doors ripped off their hinges, and walls were torn apart. The streets were deserted, not a soul was in sight, the fear and panic that once filled the streets was gone, replaced by a heavy silence, an eerie calm, the sound of nothing was ominous. We swept through the town and found nothing, no sign of hostiles, no civilians in need. The whole time the overbearing horror played in my mind, what happened to Natasha and her family, we were on the very border of the town, maybe she'd got out, to safety. Maybe they were all gone, just like the rest of the town.

"This place is a ghost town, Sarge." I radioed back to the base.

"The drone's not picking anything up either, stay on alert, the beasts could still be there." Sarge was watching the screen from the monitor back at Fort Zaffre.

"Yes Ma'am." I nodded to the rest of the group and we continued.

The main road was desolate, the houses had crumbled to rubble, the shops were abandoned, no one was home, no signs of life, the place was deserted. We reached the edge of town and closer to my house, the Kinsley Farm, the sound of the birds had gone, the farm always had a rattle of birds, squeaking and chirping, it was too much, hearing nothing. The dirt path led up to the farm all the way to Natasha's house. The whole time I was apprehensive, cautious and dreading each step, Every step brought me closer to an answer, an answer I wasn't ready to hear.

"Moretti, are you okay? You're shaking." Jameson took my hand, his grasp was firm and warm, it gave me a moment to regain composure.

"I'll be fine." I shook my head and took a deep breath, the smell was still in the air, the dust and blood was shocking, the heat wasn't helping, my head was spinning, the knot in my stomach was still there, I wasn't sure if I was dehydrated or in shock, torn between dread and determination.

"Do you want to go back?" He was concerned, his eyes were fixated on mine.

"No. I can't leave. Not without knowing." My determination was clear, my focus was set, the fear had subsided, for now.

"If you're sure. I'll be here." Jameson's eyes softened, he understood.

We headed up the path, the trees were still teeming with life, the farm was intact, but there were no signs of life. Strange black vines covered the dirt road leading to Natasha house, Wet and slimy, they covered everything.

"What the hell are these?" Church was fascinated, her hand caressed the vines, it was cold, "some kind of plant."

"Whatever they are, they are everywhere." I dashed down the road following the vines, they intertwined and wrapped around the path, covering cars, lamp posts and walls, hell it got so thick, it completely covered the dirt path. I stopped running when the house was in view.

"You've stopped." Church was out of breath, her hair was messy and stuck to her forehead.

"The vines stop here." The house was untouched, the vines hadn't reached it yet.

"That's odd." Church's voice was low and curious, "It's as if they're protecting the house."

"Natasha. Natasha!" I yelled at the top of my lungs,

I ran into the house, what I saw took me back and shocked me to my core, Officer William and Lilly in neat piles of limbs, next to each other, blood pooling under them.

"Jesus Christ." Jameson gagged, the sight was horrific, a mangled mess of body parts.

"Lilly." My voice cracked, "Natasha?" I collapsed to the floor, tears rolled down my face, I was broken.

Natasha wasn't there. She wasn't at the house, the room was a mess,the chairs were upturned, the table was on its side, curtains were torn off the railings.

"I'm sorry, Moretti. Maybe she made it out." Em tried to comfort me, but her words were hollow.

"Where is she? Where the hell is she?" I yelled, my hands shook, the anger was boiling over, my emotions were all over the place, "Where the hell is Natasha!" I booted the coffee table which slammed into the separation wall, it left a good dent. That's when I noticed it. Lettering in blood revealed the words, words that haunt me, as an old man I can still see the blood fresh and thick.

'Moretti! I have what you're looking for"

The Price that Innocent Pay

The damsel in distress

When innocence is shattered,
And cruelty takes control,
Their cries echo in the night,
They suffer an endless fight.

We must stand up for the voiceless,
Fight for justice and for truth,
Protect the innocent and defenceless,
Show compassion and share our youth.

For when the innocent are tortured,
We must not turn a blind eye,
We must speak out and be bold,
And never let their souls die.

The journey was long and arduous, on foot they trudged and dragged themselves for days. As heaps of limbs and bone they moved in a swaying motion, slowly and in time with each other, as if they were one. Miles separated Saint Morgan and Pazandir's lair on opposite corners of the map, through sand and stone, each forest larger than the previous one. Natasha, still bound by a bloodied bind, had no choice, a slave to her masters, the journey slowly broke her. Her feet blistered and bled, she had no shoes, the rocks cut deep into her soles. The torturous image of her parents demise, the beasts breaking their bodies and using them as puppets, the sight of her binds made her sick. Natasha's memories kept her going however, thoughts of Sebastian and their favourite spot beside the creek, Milo and his daft smile, playing in the shallow water. Natasha's memories often faded in and out, reminding her of the life she once had. She knew Sebastian would come, save her from her horrors.

The walking abominations, never relenting, never fading, walked as the sun rose in the sky and settled to night, days passed without rest for food or water. Natasha's strength waned, her pace slowed. The creatures would not wait for her, her only chance was to break free, to run as fast as she could, but she didn't, she couldn't. Bound and exhausted, the only thing Natasha could do was continue the slow march, the thought of Sebastian never far away.

"Please, stop! Please!"

Natasha's cries were met with no response, not even a glance. They just continued to march.

"Water! I need water, please! I can't keep walking. Please, I beg you."

Her throat was parched, her stomach rumbled and growled, the taste of iron and dust filled her mouth. A hunger she had never experienced. The abominations would not stop, not until they reached their destination. Natasha, at the very least, wanted to know where she was being taken.

"Where are we going?" she said, her voice a mere whisper.

"You will see. When we reach our destination, all shall be revealed. Pazandir is waiting!" One of the grunts grew tired of Natasha's whining, responding to her constant questioning.

With a heavy heart and a tired mind, she walked for many more days, her body broken and torn. The sun was relentless, beating down upon her exposed back, her skin cracked and dry, blisters formed causing searing pain.

After an eternity they had finally arrived, a terrifying structure carved from stone and marble. Pazandir's castle was unlike any castle Natasha had seen before. It was huge, towers of black and red pierced the skies. A long and winding staircase led from the ground to the front door, spiralling in several turns, coiling in a jagged, irregular circle.

As they made their way up the stairs Natasha glanced down at the moat surrounding the castle. Blood not water filled the moat, bodies floated by, their faces frozen in death. The stench was awful, sour and heavy, thick with ripeness, it made even the strongest stomach gag.

"The smell. Oh, gods, the smell," Natasha said as she reached for her mouth covering her senses

The entrance was large, a wide doorway that seemed to lead to an equally wide corridor. At each side of the doorway there stood a statue of a woman holding a bowl, a flame burning brightly within. Natasha looked closer at the statues, their eyes held fear and terror as they stood holding the bowls. Natasha gasped as she realised the horror, The statues came to life, animated. The sounds of chains clanged as they shifted weight, bound to welcome visitors for eternity.

"Do not fear, they will not harm you," Pazandir said as he watched her. "They are here to show how great my power is. If I want something to be still, then it shall be. They will remain chained for all eternity. Their only task is to show how great I am."

His sinister grin engulfed his face as he spoke, he enjoyed and revelled in the torment of others, pride was evident in his voice. Natasha shuddered, the power to bind a creature into eternal servitude was utter evil in its purest form.

"Now, if you will, please enter, we have much to discuss" the voice bellowed from the skies.

"We have arrived, my pet," A beast spoke, the snake-like demon grinned, its tongue lapped frantically.

Natasha looked up, her eyes sunken and dull, her once vibrant and strong body had faded, leaving her thin and sickly. With torn clothes her will was tested, She did not reply, her voice was broken and raspy, dry and sore from the desert sands, lost somewhere along the way. Pazandir lifted her, his scaly arms carried her, with long sharp claws grazing her skin.

"The time has come to fulfil your destiny, and when I have what I want, I will let you die, I will make you whole again, and set you free," The beast spoke a deep guttural growl followed by a sharp hiss, his tongue weaved in and out between his teeth.

"he must be slain by my hand and you, you are the key to gaining his attention"

Natasha did not resist, there was nothing left of her, nothing left but a shell.

The demon placed Natasha on the ground, her hands and legs still bound, the demon pulled out a dagger.

"Let us send him a gift," The demon said.

He brought the blade to her chest, an ornate weapon of gold and steel, delicate carvings of a snake wrapped around a wolf, its grip tight as it slowly syphoned its life. The blade had magical properties, it could take the lifeforce of its victim without fully killing them. The demon cut deeply, slicing open the skin, blood trickled slowly, she could feel her heart race frantically, her lungs filled with air as she gasped in pain.

"I have made you. Return, so that you may do my bidding," the beast said.

"When your body is ready, you will be the instrument of my revenge," It added.

She was still alive, she could feel her soul cling to the good, but the pain was too strong. She closed her eyes and screamed in agony.

"You will live, as long as I need you to," the beast hissed.

"You will be mine, my queen, we shall rule this land and become one, once we vanquish your prince, that is" the beast roared.

"Sebastian," Natasha called for her love, but her voice was too weak and frail.

The demon lifted the blade high, he grinned as his plan came to fruition, his jagged sharp teeth overwhelmed his face with layers of pincers like a shark. His eyes glowed red with anger and envy, he remembered the feeling of want, the feeling of love and respect, he could see Natasha's total and complete dependence on Sebastian as she lay helpless, calling out his name. He wanted it, all of it, to be loved and respected by the humans again. The beast knew not the power of a soul, and the strength it had, even when the body had given in, the spirit of a person is unbreakable.

"I will break your will" the demon hissed.

"You will become what you were destined to be, a tool, a weapon, a vessel of destruction, the very thing you have been fighting for centuries. I will use you to destroy everything you love, I will end the human race," the beast yelled. He gripped his blade tight with a furious rage and cut deep, severing bone, separating limb from body.

She stared deep into the beast's eyes with anger and might, her love for Sebastian was deep and true. She took her time and mustered her strength,

"He will come and you will suffer the wrath of his might" she spoke, her voice a faint whisper.

The beast laughed and roared. "Your will is broken, I have won!" the beast said.

"Never," Natasha replied.

The demon smiled, its mouth curled. He reached for a contraption, a torture device of pure evil.

"We shall see your strength"

With a heavy hand, he pushed Natasha into the ground splaying her arms and legs wide, he grabbed his blade with might and lust as he carved his finest creation. Reaching into her ribcage he opened her chest, her body convulsed in pain, Pazandir made sure she felt each moment as he deformed her. Constructing wings from her ribs he muttered incantations to bring them to life,

"Zire-nansaa madikaa...bijamali"

He continued the process, splitting her femur and tibia, a four legged beast he morphed her into his perfect creature. His spell was nearing completion, he would make his pet into the most powerful creature of his imagination.

"Zire-nansaa man 'antaas...bijamali"

Natasha's eyes, wide and scared, she sobbed and cried as her body fell limp and deformed, her legs were split apart and her wings, her monstrous wings were made to flap as they lifted her off the ground. The beast had turned her into a creature of nightmare, a four legged winged dragon. She screamed, her voice a mix of agony and despair, the transformation was near complete. He finally reached violently down her throat and yanked sharply at her chords, each ripping under the pressure, the ferocious attack causing her to scream like a banshee. Pazandir had almost completed the transformation, he just needed to add one final touch, to seal the spell forever. The demon reached behind Natasha's ear and whispered a secret, an ancient curse.

"Vespero Bijamali"

"Rise, rise my child," the demon said.

Natasha sprung to life, she twitched and spasmed as her mind adjusted to the abomination, her body was different, stronger, faster, and her wings, she could feel them move. She was not human anymore, she had been transformed into a beast made for one purpose, destruction.

"Look at me," the demon commanded.

Natasha looked at him, her eyes now a vivid red, she could see his soul, the anger and hate he held. Her mind was different, clearer, her body was a machine, an apex predator.

"What have you done to me?" Natasha asked.

"You are the key, a vessel, a weapon, the instrument of my vengeance," the beast said. "You will bring him to me"

Natasha's mind was not her own, a force stronger than her, her body moved as the demon commanded. She had no control over her movements, no say in her decisions.

She was a slave to Pazandir, a servant, a puppet of evil. Her body was his and his alone, her will broken, her spirit defeated.

"Fly," the beast said.

Her wings spread wide, her body light.

"Faster, higher" the beast commanded.

Her speed and height increased, she flew fast and true. The wind rushed through her, the freedom she felt, the exhilaration was like nothing she had ever experienced. She flew with might and precision, a predator searching for prey, the desire to hunt was overwhelming.

"Kill" the beast commanded.

The Need for Answers

When times are difficult

Through darkness and doubt they tread,
Carrying the burdens on their head.
But deep within, a flame still burns,
A flicker of hope that fiercely yearns.

Will my hero fall to despair,
In the face of trials unfair?
Will he crumble under the weight,
Or rise above it, never to abate?

And though the path may be unclear
We know the hero will persevere
to rise above the shadows deep
and claim the victory we seek.

Sounds fell silent, the taste of dry bitter ash added to the nausea and cold sweats, my world, upside down. Those words rang through my mind like a pounding drum, the blood still dripped, she wasn't far. Natasha was all alone and held captive, Why? Questions raced, making me dizzy. Why target me? Do I chase whoever did this? Which direction? What beast caused this much chaos? Jameson had to take over, I was in no fit state to lead a team, not effectively anyway.

"We've swept the area, let's get back to base and report our findings, we need to strategize and deploy accordingly" Jameson wasn't bad, I underestimated his leadership skills, maybe even better than me, at least an excellent second in command. He Picked me up from my knees and called in for a Humvee pick up, they must have known and stood by close, arriving within three minutes. "Called in for a pickup, Zaffre or Gamboge?" The driver must have done several laps, back and forth deploying units, surrounding the Saint Morgan area.
"Zaffre!" Church called out as Jameson checked my mental state. I must have been out of it, lost in a daze, going by the look in his eyes,

"Bro, Moretti!" He shook me a few times, snapping me out a daze "Stay with me pal, we'll get her back, we need to find out what the fuck these shits are, I got your back. We'll find her!" His words pulled my sorry ass together, no point gazing into the distance, feeling sorry for myself, picturing the worst case scenario. I needed to step up. I wiped away my tears, my hands rested on the back of the humvee seat in front. I felt the heat and sweat in my palms. I had no idea how the hell we were going to fight off these monsters, having no idea what they were, where they came from or what they were after, we needed answers. I hoped someone from base camp could enlighten us, somebody should've known more than us. I didn't want to go the old fashioned route and hit the books, endlessly searching through fairy tales and stories of mythology. It would've taken too long. I was right.

The trip was fast, no more than fifteen minutes, the driver must have broken a few laws. Hell, No cops were in sight so who gave a shit, I'm pretty sure the military over-ranks local police anyways.

The sun had gone down, it was dark outside, the only lights were from the search teams and helicopters. It was quiet and solemn, the whole town was eerily still, no more gunfire, no screaming.

When the humvee stopped, at the gates, he swung a u-turn ready to make the journey again.

"Good luck" was the last thing he said.

The gates were wide open, teams flooding in and out, they were still deploying, some were coming in by air from Gamboge, I guess their base camp was running a helicopter drop off and pick up service, smart.

When we entered, the whole area lit up. One of the sergeants was directing the traffic, Humvees picking up equipment and fuel, the Ammo boxes were left untouched, nobody actually firing at anything meant no real threat...for the moment. Sergeant Ackerman flagged us over, she was on the top floor in the main building, one of the offices. I reckon she was waiting for us, hoping to get more intel, funny, we needed the same.

"Glad you made it, I was getting worried" she greeted, her voice was soft and welcoming, the tone changed when she looked at me.

"Moretti, what's wrong?" Ackerman knew me well enough, she'd overseen a few training sims and conducted a few mental psyche tests to know what made me tick, the whole time I never lost my composure.

"My Girl, Fiance" I couldn't find the correct words, I showed her the footage from my bodycam, she paused, her expression changed, it was a mix of sadness and anger.

"Moretti!" her hand squeezed my shoulder as she saw the message in blood, I felt the warmth and comfort, I wasn't alone, not completely, "We need to find out what we are dealing with, I'll get a message to the whole base, I want you guys to head to the archives in the base library, we may get lucky"

"Roger, Ma'am" Jameson was quick to the punch.

We headed to the library, the archives were locked away behind a secure door, guarded by two armed marines.

"Sir, you can't come in, these are top secret" One of the guards had a hard expression, his body language was stiff and tense, I'm guessing he was a new recruit.

"Moretti, Sector C, I've got the all clear from My Sarge" The guard seemed to know, he stepped aside and opened the door.

"Thanks," I nodded in appreciation. He was just doing his job, which made my life easier.

The archives were dark and dusty, the walls were lined with books and papers, three floors of floor to ceiling classified archives. Wooden archways lead a path through the labyrinth of knowledge. The musty smell of mothballs and mould made the whole place reek of decay. The flickering lights from the candles placed in each alcove dimly lit the area, just enough to see and navigate my way around. The rickety old floorboards creaked with every step, I would have found it funny, if the circumstances were different.

"Let's get reading!" Em was first to the drawers, "I'll take the files"

"Jameson and I will take the books." Church grabbed Jameson and grabbed a pile of books, slamming them on the dusty table.

We were surrounded by papers, books and reports, I couldn't read the dates, they were too old and the ink had faded.

"What's the year on this file, Em?" Jameson was the first to ask, his voice was tired and raspy, I felt the same.

"Looks like 1870" Church answered, she was the first to crack a book, "It's going to be a long night"

I separated from the group, still in ear shot, I reckon they would make their way through that section and come find me. The section on ancient myths caught my attention. Nothing of value, just old tales, stories passed from generations, probably fabricated and edited each time it passed from one to another. I had no clue why the hell these books were classified. Then I found it, the spine was laced in gold with bloodied lettering 'Zakariah the good' squeezed between 'Demons of hell' and 'The end times', the book was worn, the edges were ripped and bent. I carefully pulled the book out, it was heavy, I was surprised that such a small book was so damn heavy. At around five by eight inches and not even an inch thick, the book weighed a good twelve kilos, I almost dropped it.

"Moretti, what did you find?" Jameson and Church made their way, they were both covered in dust and cobwebs, looking like they had no luck with their books.

"Not sure, looks old" I flipped open the cover.

Zakariah the Good

Inner Demons

It whispers dark thoughts into minds of the weak,
Turning their souls black, making them bleak.
It feeds on their fears, their doubts and despair,
Leaving them helpless, trapped in its snare.

But we must not give in to this evil force,
We must stand strong, stay on our course.
For in the light of love and truth we'll find,
The power to banish this demon from our mind.

So let us band together, in unity and might,
And drive this demon back into the night.
For we are strong, we are brave, we are true,
And with courage and faith, we will see it through

In the darkest depths, far from Saint Morgan an evil force lay dormant. It was a slumbering thing, barely sentient, and yet it dreamt. In its dreams, it heard the screams of a child, and felt a strange sense of loss. The thirst of power and dominance awoke. It sensed that a being like itself, a being who was a void in the world, had been created. And like was calling to like.

An unnatural army called the beasts of shadow, slowly began to gather. Abominations of horror formed, grotesque beings of blood and bone, of flesh and magic. Some were made of nothing more than mist and shadow and hatred.

A horde of terror rose from the earth as their master slept, preparing to awaken him. With destruction, they conquered lands and their power grew. Hatred, blood lust and greed fueled their growing numbers and their strength. Covering towns and villages, the horror swept lands afar. The people fought the beasts but they could not win. They could not destroy them. So, as the horror reached their doorsteps the people fled. Abandoning homes and cities, leaving all behind.

Pazandir, the bringer of destruction and keeper of time born from ash and stone, rose from the depths of hell. A greater call empowered his thirst and with his power he called forth a great storm. Pazandir's fury was glorious and the lands were devoured. He would stop at nothing to destroy all that was good and light. The demon had not a physical form but a spiritual presence, not of flesh but a manifestation of evil and malice. Born of two forms, the all powerful immortal god, that lingered and influenced evil within creatures, controlling them like puppets and the earth form, a beast , tall and gangly, with giant horns and thick scaly skin. He commanded his armies and controlled storms.

The great storm raged across the land, as the people cried for a saviour. The storm brought devastation and death, fire and flood, and then came the beasts. Their howls echoed on the winds, as they were carried to the farthest corners of the world. All hope seemed lost. The people were without a protector, and had no way of stopping the storms or the creatures that came with it. The people prayed, Their prayers were unanswered.

—

Pazandir was once human, he was once good. From the ancient lands of Monazite, long before the city was built, and far before the great war, Pazandir was once the leader of a great tribe. He was born with the ability to hear the dead, a prophet and the leader of his people.

For years, he ruled the lands with wisdom and justice, but Pazandir began to grow tired and frustrated. The world had changed, the people were not the same. Filled with greed and hate for one another, they fought wars and slaughtered their neighbours. The world was in chaos, the people did not heed the words of the wise oracle.

"In a world full of negativity and despair, Let's choose peace, No place for violence, no room for fear Let's stand together"

Pazandir could see that the future of the world was dark and full of despair, the end of all life was near. Pazandir was finally driven mad, he turned his back on the world. Growing tired of the warring, the greed, the violence, the evil, the suffering and pain. He would end it all. He travelled to the birthplace of his tribe and made an offer to the gods, Climbing forty thousand steps to the peak of the mountain where a small chapel sat tucked within the cliffs, Pazandir trudged with each step, his muscles getting heavier and heavier. Reaching the top was no easy feat. Pazandir took the last step and was in awe of the holy presence, the sweat on his forehead had turned to ice, large salty crystals sporadically formed, clumps of ice in his long hair and beard. Upon entering the chapel he sacrificed his powers of good and offered his soul as payment, turning to evil. He accepted the gift of the gods and used it against humanity, with the aim to right the wrongs, the warring and suffrage. It was then that Pazandir became the bringer of destruction.

With all great evils must be a greater good, A light that shines brighter in the darkness.

A young child was born, the son of the king and queen, a boy whose destiny was already set in stone. For the child's soul was ancient and had seen all. He was the chosen one, a warrior born to save the world, The ancestor of Sebastian Moretti. The child was named Zakariah. The King and Queen of Azurite knew their child would have a great destiny, so they kept the prophecy a secret and told no one. As Zakariah grew older, he began to notice that his mind was different. He was more gifted than other children, he was stronger, faster and smarter than the average boy. Zakariah was a very sensitive and loving child. He would often see things in his dreams and visions. He was able to see and hear things that others could not, memories of the dead. Zakariah would often tell his mother about his dreams, tales of love and loss, stories of adventure and horrors of war, Understandably Zakariah's mother became concerned for the boy, seeking help, she researched these dreams and discovered the truth, real life accounts from civilizations far from Azurite.

Zakariah came of age and joined the forces of good to battle the bringer of destruction, the beasts of shadow, and the minions of evil.

Zakariah, a knight, a warrior, a hero and a champion, was destined to be the bringer of balance, the one who would stand up against the evil that threatened the world, on the eve of battle, he stood before the enemy, his armour shining in the moonlight. He faced Pazandir, the bringer of destruction, as they clashed swords, a bright light burst from Zakariah's blade, blinding the enemy, with the enemy rendered blind, Zakariah lunged his blade deep into the beast and put an end to Pazandir's reign of terror, sending the beast to a deep slumber. Zakariah had succeeded, he had saved the world from destruction,

Unfortunately and unknowingly fulfilling the prophecy and fusing the two souls together.

As time passed, and after a long and happy life Zakariah's soul returned to the afterlife, the people began to forget about him and his deeds, they began to live their lives and forget the dark times that once was.

A legend foretold, a story passed down through generations, the tale of the hero and his battle against evil. A story of bravery and sacrifice, of love and loss.

—

Unfortunately, history has a way of repeating itself, the birth of Sebastian and the awakening of his soul also disturbed the soul of Pazandir. Evil brewed beneath the earth waiting for a time to strike and return to power.

The world is once more facing the darkness of old, a darkness so thick and strong it can not be destroyed by steel or stone, no cast of a spell or a well placed arrow, but a great sacrifice, a sacrifice from a greater good. It will test his might, test his will. Only he has the answer.

Steel Yourself

Espionage

On a secret mission to save the world,
We will need friends to help us unfurl.
Together we'll fight against darkness and fear,
Protecting all that we hold dear.

Their strength and courage will be our guide,
Standing by our side, they'll never hide.
In unity we'll face the challenges ahead,
With unwavering resolve, no fear or dread.

With loyalty and trust, we'll face the storm,
United we'll conquer, our purpose will form.
On this secret mission, united we stand,
With our friends at our side, we'll protect the land

The pages were thin and fragile, A story of great evil and sacrifice, the events and horrors matched those in Saint Morgan, I feared this was the answer to all our questions.

"Anything?" Em was eager, her eyes were fixated on the pages, she read over my shoulder.

"It's talking about a war, a war that destroyed the world" Jameson's eyes widened.

"Wait, what?" Church was confused, "There is no evidence of such a war."

"Look." I turned the page and showed her. The image of a winged beast fighting hordes of men as Zakariah vanquished the demon from hell.

"I'll call it in, the rest of the teams should hear this" Em dashed off, quicker than a flash.

"This book tells of a menacing war, a war that lasted for years" I was hesitant to continue, my words were slow and cautious.

If it wasn't for the similarities I would have pegged it for a tale, a storybook written to entertain folk around a campfire, nothing more. Still the monstrosities were similar enough for us to report them up the chain of command, let them deal with the validity.

"Well, there's no other lead," I made my way out, The book was tightly grasped under my arm. I wasn't looking forward to the meeting, not with the state of things.

The walk was slow and awkward, the teams had gathered in the mess hall, the chatter was low and hushed. We entered the office, Sergeant Ackerman was already in a discussion with the Colonel, a stern and worried expression slapped on both their faces, they weren't pleased with the situation, not in the slightest.

"Sergeant Ackerman" I addressed my sergeant, her attention snapped, her eyes fixed on me.

"Moretti, good. Report!"

I told them everything, the story, the monster, the blood. I didn't hold back, not that I had much of a choice.

"Well, that explains the lack of information in the archives, it's a story, nothing more" the Colonel was quick to dismiss it, "Get rid of it!"

"Sir, no. It's worth investigating, we've got a team that is willing to go and look"

"No, we don't have the resources or the manpower. I'm calling off the search."

"Sir?" We were stunned.

"We have no information, no idea what the fuck we are dealing with, this could be the end of humanity, a story is not enough, the risk is too high."

"I'm going, sir!" I protested.

"No, you're not. We need experienced soldiers, not a love struck kid. This is an order. I'm ordering the withdrawal of the troops, we are falling back. Fortifying the barracks."

"But..."

"Moretti! This is an order."

"Moretti. Don't, we have our orders." Sarge cut in, interrupting me, saving me from a court martial.

"Yes, Sir."

I walked out, my legs were shaking, my knees weak. I felt sick, it was a nightmare, the Colonel was wrong. I knew it, but orders were orders.

"Moretti, we have to get ready." Em was at my side, she had overheard the whole conversation.

"You're right, let's move, just us"

"Are you sure?"

"I've got no other choice, I've got to do something, I've got to try, if only for her"

"Let's go." Em was a good friend, I'm glad she was on my side, not a moment did she hesitate, she didn't flinch, not once.

We had to pack light, enough supplies to last a few days, food, water and ammo. We had the night to ourselves, no one was stopping us, I reckon the Colonel was happy to be rid of us, one less thing to worry about. Jameson and Church overheard us in the locker room, they were quick to join us, I was glad, no questions asked.

"Moretti, what are we packing, how many days do you think we are going for?" Jameson was keen, he was quick to gather up his equipment, loading it into a humvee, one of the drivers left the key in the ignition, a mistake he'd pay for later.

"Not sure, maybe a few days, I'm not sure how far they got but we'll catch em in this, it's all up to the book, the map shows exactly where Pazandir is" I replied,

"Let's load up, Moretti, I'm driving, we need you focused" Church called out.

We were set. I took one step in the Humvee and felt dizzy, the world went dark, a chill in the air flashed over me like a wave. Yichén's voice echoed, "Moretti, pay a visit to my kinsmen, they're in Azurite City, it's on the way, The Shíjiān Warriors. You need help."

"Moretti?" Em shouted, her words echoed, her face was blurred.

"I'm ok,"

"Maybe we should wait till morning"

"No, no, I'm fine." I continued, Yichén's words raced through my mind, maybe he was right, fighting a horde of demons with four rookie soldiers was a little foolish to say the least, even if we had powers, we were no match.

The engine roared and the lights blazed a trail, the trip was fast, with no traffic and no stops. The road was straight and open, with not a person in sight, it was eerily quiet,

"I need to make a detour, It's in the right direction," I made the call, Yichén never failed me and was wise, listening to my guide was part of the training sim, the ability to take the leap of faith and trust the word of a stranger.

"Ok, Moretti. Where to?" Church was the first to answer.

"Azurite city,"

"Azurite City?" Em had a confused look on her face, she never questioned my decisions until now. "Why?"

"We need reinforcements" I said with faith, having no idea what that meant.

"Jameson, stay on comms, keep an ear on the Colonel" I called out. "Any sign of the Colonel catching wind of us and our timeline is fucked"

"Got it, Moretti" Jameson was quick,

The humvee roared on, we were going at speed, the headlights flashed on the signs, Azurite City was getting closer, the sprawling cityscape lit up like a christmas tree, the city never slept, it made me feel uneasy, a farm boy like me never belonged in the city, I wasn't ready for the fast paced, hectic life of a big city.

We parked in a dark alleyway, not too close, not too far, just in case we had to make a quick escape. The Shíjiān Warriors had control over Chinatown, they probably already knew we were coming, their reputation for spying and information gathering was renowned, they'd have their eyes on the whole city.

"Ok, you three, stay here. Keep the engine running, if anything happens, we have an escape route. I'll be in and out, no more than 30 minutes." The front entrance was just around the corner, steps elevated to a glass rotary door, two Asian guards stood proud and emotionless, the building from the outside wasn't too extravagant, just another end terrace three-story house, dark red brick with black PVC windows, each window had a bright red wind chime which glowed in a pulsing fashion. Their use of magic was sophisticated and they weren't scared to let everyone know, magical wards like that meant only one thing, protection from unwanted guests.

The street was empty, the lights above the door and windows were the only light source, I walked around the corner and headed for the front door. As I approached the door the guards swivelled, pivoting to let me by, *'Madame Zhou is waiting, take the elevator to the top.'* I had expected some form of security, the lack of any check or screening was alarming.

I walked through the rotary doors and into the front room, white marble floors with monochrome furniture, pops of vivid red items placed thoughtfully around the room, a lampshade, a fruit bowl, the plant pot in the corner all to make me feel at ease, that was far from the truth. Madame Zhou expected me and was waiting. I couldn't spend too much time soaking up the decor of the establishment, so I headed up the central stairway and into the elevator. The penthouse floor was already highlighted. It surprised me a little, maybe the controls were external, operated by one of Zhou's minions. The doors opened to the penthouse suite, three ladies played string instruments in the corner of the room, sweet and soft their melodies were soothing and helped ease my anxiety. Madame Zhou was in the middle of the room, her hair, jet black and straight, falling down her shoulders and resting on her chest, her makeup, bold, lips the colour of a blood red rose, dark kohl and heavy eyelashes, fluttering like butterflies. Ornate Gold statues stood between pillars all facing the long walkway. Madame Zhou was clearly a fan of the male anatomy, the statues were carved into different positions, all naked, caricatures and exaggerations of real life men.

I walked the length of the room and stopped in front of Madame Zhou, she sat there unfazed and unamused, dressed in a gold and black cheongsam, her arms were bare, a black band adorned her upper arm, it glowed with the same pulse as the windchimes outside, her hands were wrapped in black lace.

"Please, sit, Mr. Moretti. We have been expecting you?" She gestured towards the chair across from her. I was not in the mood for games, I was there for one reason, one purpose.

"Mr Moretti it is customary for guests to have a drink before proceeding with business, It is the finest vintage." Madame Zhou had a glass of deep red wine in her hand, her nails were painted to match. She had a sultry tone, almost hypnotic and seductive.

"Thank you, but no. I have no time, I have come for aid, we face a great evil, we need help" I was adamant, the wine was obviously spiked, the girls in the room were not just for entertainment, their music was enchanting, they were a part of a greater scheme, Zhou was playing games.

"I know what you have come for. Your quest is noble, but I do not wish to get involved, the Shíjiān warriors have remained neutral since the founding, we will continue this way."

"You have no choice, Pazandir, the bringer of destruction has risen. The world needs you."

"You are a man of strong ideals and belief, Mr. Moretti, however the Shíjiān Warriors remain neutral, we do not wish to involve ourselves in the matters of the outside world.

"This is no ordinary fight, The world will fall if we don't stop him, the world will die, no magic, no technology, the end of times is upon us."

"If this is true, then we will face our fate, if not, we will continue the way we are." Madame Zhou had no emotion, her words were cold, I could not convince her, she was resolute.

"Yichén sent me, he said you'd help"

Zhou's eyes darted towards me in shock, "How do you know that name!"

"I can speak to the dead, they guide me and show me the future" I explained everything, It felt like the only path to getting her on my side.

"If this is true, what was his first gift to me?" Zhou was testing me, testing my connection to Yichén. I waited for

Yichén to speak, he fed me information as and when I needed it.

"A single Violet Rose, he plucked it from the Nanjing gardens, it is how he introduced himself to you."

"And what did he say?" I had a feeling she knew, she just wanted to hear it again. Her love for Yichén was strong, the loss must have cut deep, I knew then meeting Yichén was fate, that his voice spoke to me for a reason. I paused and spoke to Yichén again.

"If eyes are the windows to the soul, then you must have the most beautiful soul, this rose is a mere fraction of your beauty"

"You are an unusual one, Mr. Moretti, Yichén was my first love, the world took him from me, a heartless act." her tone softened, her guard lowered. "If we help you, we help you for him. We will need a favour first"

"What kind of favour"

"Our enemies are the Red Dragons, the leader of the Red Dragons has taken something from us. We want you to retrieve it"

"What have they taken?"

"They took our honour, They stole our secrets, our history. A book, the book you need to aid your quest. They have taken the secrets of the Shíjiān Warriors."

"I'll take care of it, where can I find them?"

"Their compound is just South, not far. They are well guarded, you will have to be clever" Zhou paused for a second, "luck, as it seems, is on our side, There is a way, a small chance, a window of opportunity"

"What do you mean?" I was bewildered, her sense of grace and superiority fell into a cunning menace.

"The Red Dragons are holding a fundraiser. You will have to attend as my guest. I will arrange a suit. When the time comes, we will have the distraction you need." Zhou came to life, animated by her excitement, her lust for justice, maybe even revenge, "The secrets of the Shíjiān Warriors are written in an ancient book, and passed down through generations. The cover has a serpent clutching a scorpion"

"I will find the book, and I will bring it back," I reassured her, we needed aid against Pazandir, I could not fail.

"Then I will grant you access to our library, place it upon the empty pedestal and restore our power. Our people will guide you"

"Perfect!"

"There is no time to waste, Mr. Moretti, your target will be at the party, Mr Kobayashi holds a private card game in his office, you will have to charm your way into the game, a wall of books behind his desk will reveal his safe." She sighed before continuing "I don't know how the safe opens, you will need to find a way in, the book will be there"

"I need to get back to my team, they'll be wondering what's going on"

"I have sent for my team to pick them up, they are getting ready as we speak, they know of our mission"

"You will escort me to the fundraiser, they will stand by as backup."

I got up to leave, and bowed respectfully to Madame Zhou. The elevator door opened and I was escorted to the lower levels. The guards waited for me outside. The room was adorned with colourful robes, vivid magenta and vermillion gowns draped over porcelain statues. A small woman approached me.

"It's good to meet you, Mr Moretti, I will take care of your attire" she spoke in a sing-song voice, I was ushered into the room and stripped bare, "My name is Su-Chan, I will take measurements and have a suit made for you, I am an expert tailor"

She wore a charcoal pinstripe suit and a black trilby hat, a red measure tape hung from her neck. She ran her hand over my body, I have to admit, it was a little uncomfortable.

"Madame Zhou has told me you are a warrior, so I have chosen a suit to match, something that will enhance your abilities, and make you more stealthy"

"I don't know how much of a stealthy guy I am, but I will try" I said with a grin.

Su-Chan measured every inch of my body, she was very thorough, and had me stand on a stool while she took measurements from all angles.

"This is perfect, It will only take a moment. My assistants will finish it and you can be on your way." she wasn't joking *'Only take a moment'* not two minutes had passed after she took my measurements "Ready!" a small squeak called out.

The suit was magnificent, a blend of the finest fabrics, a matte black fabric which clung to my legs, it's stretchy material flexed with ease and was light enough to allow easy movement, the jacket was made of a soft yet durable fabric, a greyish tint, and had a shimmer when the light caught it. It was the perfect combination of fashion and functionality, Su-Chan really did a remarkable job. I'd never bought a suit before, never had any need, I'd never gone to any fancy occasions to need one. That's when I'd remembered, this whole time, I was living it up, getting a fancy suit tailored, all the while Natasha was gone, lost and in danger. My heart sank, the heavy knot in my throat sank and made it hard to swallow.

"What's wrong Mr Moretti? Not to your liking?" Su-Chan looked shocked, I got the feeling she always hit the mark.

"It's great, I love it, I'm just distracted." I didn't want to offend her.

"Wearing this, you'll have the whole room distracted, It is a work of art," She brushed my sleeve, removing the lint "The pants are a new fabric, I call it Poly-Silk" She ruffled my hair and frowned "Need to sort this out"

"I've always worn my hair like this." I didn't want a haircut. I felt my natural curly mess was charming, and gave me a humble, wholesome look.

"Oh no, I can't have you leaving here looking like this, not with Madame Zhou. You'll be the talk of the town"

She guided me into a chair and started cutting my hair. Her handiwork was impressive, she had an eye for detail, and her skills were remarkable. The cut was short and sharp, clean and professional. It made me feel confident, powerful, the mirror in front of me showed a new man, a more refined and sophisticated person. She styled a slick pompadour with a high bald fade, and trimmed my beard to contour my face shape.

"Much better," she said, standing back and admiring her work, "A suiter for Madame Zhou"

"It's perfect. Thank you" I bowed and made my way back to the lobby, a black limo was parked perfectly in front of the door, polished to a mirror finish, with chrome wheels with angular designs and tinted windows, as black as the body's paint the door swung open. Madame Zhou waved me in "Looking good Mr Moretti"

"Thank you, It was the work of a genius" I replied.

"Your team is waiting in the next block, they will be with us every step of the way" Zhou handed me an earpiece. It was so small I was concerned about losing it in my ear, it fit like a glove.

The back was spacious, with a large sunroof and two seats facing each other, a drinks cabinet stocked with champagne and a selection of fine spirits. The leather seats were black and smooth, cool to the touch.

"To the fundraiser"

"On our way, Madame"

"So, What's the plan"

"I will work the room, greet the guests and work my way around the lobby, you will accompany me," She placed her hand on my thigh "Be charming and witty, most importantly be complementary, these people love to hear how wonderful they are"

"Ok, I can do that"

"My assistant will stay at the bar, if anyone starts asking too many questions, she will let me know"

"Sounds good"

"The office will be guarded, Those invited or asked to play a private game with Mr Kobayashi are allowed in" This was gonna be the hard part, gaining trust from a complete stranger, enough trust that he leads me into his private office. It all sounded far-fetched.

"Madame Zhou, if I may? If the Red Dragons are sworn enemies, why are you invited to a fundraiser? And, If we are seen...Together, then why would Mr Kobayashi want me anywhere near him, that would be a huge security risk, right?" Zhou giggled and shifted her body to face me, she tucked my hair behind my ear, "Keep your friends close, your enemies...closer" She leaned in to kiss me, her lips soft and moist, I pulled backwards into my seat regretfully ending the kiss, It took all my strength, she was gorgeous. Her red silk dress hugged her curvaceous body, with gold delicate embroidery and fine detailing on her left shoulder. For an older woman, she was stunning, hell, she was stunning regardless.

"I have a girlfriend, please, let's keep this professional"

"Impressive Mr Moretti, I admire that." her expression changed, and her tone was softer, she was no longer the powerful, dominating and manipulative figure I'd met.

"I'm sorry, it's just. My girlfriend is missing, She's trapped somewhere, I need to save her"

"My apologies, Mr. Moretti. However, tonight you need to concentrate on the mission at hand, no distractions, people need to see us as a young and happy couple in love." She looked at me with a genuine smile. "If it's any consolation, Yichén would approve."

"I'm sure he would, He was a great man"

The Red Dragon Fundraiser

The Hero faces a test

Silent footsteps in the night,
A stealthy figure out of sight,
Creeping through the shadows deep,
Into the enemy's base I leap.

Heart pounding in my chest,
Every nerve put to the test,
Adrenaline fuels my bold advance,
As I take a risky chance.

So I press on, undaunted, undismayed,
In the darkness, I make my way,
For in the end, victory will be sweet,
When I emerge victorious, my mission complete.

"We're here" The car slowed down, eventually coming to a stop. We drove at a snail pace, cruising around the city, flaunting our attendance and ensuring our fashionably late arrival. The doors unlocked and we were greeted by a valet. Zhou linked her arm around mine, I was still uneasy, this was a risky mission. I tried not to think about it, get my head into the role. The red carpet led the way to the steps in front of the towering mansion, large floor to ceiling windows covered the walls, little alcoves made space for tea lights that lit up the building, the ambiance was perfect, classy with a touch of sexy. The clambering bodies pushed and shoved each other on both sides of us, the rope barrier looked flimsy and far too thin to hold them back, every time one of them would get too close they'd receive a cold sharp jolt. Their flashing lights blinded me as they desperately took pictures. I gave them all something to focus on, reaching my hand I gently placed it on Zhou's hip, I pulled her in closer, her heels made her almost as tall as me. Her grip was tight and firm, her fingers wrapped around my head, pulling the two of us close, a smile spread across her face. It was a picture perfect shot, we kissed for a good few seconds. The flashes continued, the reporters and paparazzi loved us. We finally entered the grand foyer, a giant chandelier caught my eye, pretty hard to miss to be honest, small spherical lanterns spiralled down getting larger as it gradually descended. The ornate floral design cast a paisley pattern on the ceiling, flames danced to the sound of the violins playing in the background. The floor was a dark marble, swirls of grey and white carved cracks into the dark cold shade of black, spotless and polished, it felt more like a showroom than a home. A huge staircase led to the upper floor, the guards were at the ready standing at the base, I watched as they checked everyone going up, only a few were let by. The bar was full, punters choosing their first shot of poison of the night, judging each other on their taste for liquor, a whiskey on the rocks meant you enjoyed your alcohol a little too much and preferred the end of the night bladdered and on the floor, a beer showed your lack of class and sophistication. Most opted for the champagne, a safe choice, their nerves settled as their moods loosened.

"We will work the room, schmooze the guests. The party will move to the ballroom, then people will filter off and the night will be over" Zhou explained.

"I'll do my best"

"Relax, remember, you're a charming and charismatic young man, who loves and respects women. You are my equal and my partner, these people need to see you as such."

"That I can do"

Zhou made her way to the centre of the room, her arms opened wide, she hugged a young woman, who must have been in her twenties. A fake hug with so little contact, it looked obvious and forced, I had no idea how these people worked, all for show and the pomp and glory, it made me sick.

"Hello darling, It's been too long" her voice was like a snake, charming and persuasive.

"Indeed it has, and who is this handsome man?" The woman looked me up and down, a judgemental stare, her eyes pierced my soul, a menacing and hateful look.

"This is my partner, Sebastian, from Cadmium City, he's a surgeon" Zhou looked at me "This is my old friend, Miss. Fletcher"

"Pleased to meet you" She held out her hand in a limp downward position. The room fell dark and cold, the guests all moved in slow motion, as if time stood still, Yichén's voice called to me "Bend at your waist, raise her hand to your lips and kiss her ring finger gently, then say 'the pleasure is all mine, Madame Zhou has spoken very dearly of you' then smile" the room warmed up, the guests walked in at a casual pace, I followed Yichén's instructions to the tee, "the pleasure is all mine, Madame Zhou has spoken very dearly of you" Miss Fletcher giggled in flattery, she blushed.

"I hope we will have the pleasure of talking again, later in the evening." She turned her attention to the crowd and moved on, disappearing amongst the sea of people.

"Very smooth" Zhou smiled, the two of us continued around the room, stopping to chat with random guests, none of which meant anything to me. Zhou seemed to know most of them. She had a talent for small talk, she worked the room with a practised grace, her charm and beauty drew them in, and her personality made them stay, she was captivating, mesmerising, I could see why people loved her, and respected her. The atmosphere was calm and relaxing, a welcome change to the constant danger and threat. I hate the fact I forgot all about Natasha.

"Madame Zhou!" A gruff male voice bellowed in surprise from across the room

"Mr Kobayashi," She replied.

"I was not expecting you to attend this evening," Kobayashi walked towards us, his hands cupped in a praying position.

"It is true that the Red Dragons and the Shíjiān Warriors are not friends, but I would never turn down an invitation, after all, it is for a good cause, is it not?"

"Absolutely, It is for a good cause." His smile was fake, a mask hiding a more sinister motive.

"Let us not talk of business, this is a party after all"

"Of course, let me have the pleasure to personally introduce you to my paramore" Zhou pulled me closer.

"Please, tell me more about yourself, Mr...?"

"Moretti"

"Mr Moretti, please"

"There isn't much to tell, I'm a doctor from Cadmium City," I had no idea what I was doing, Zhou was leading the way, and I followed.

"Ah, I see, and how did you two love birds meet?"

The room faded again, Yichén spoke to me "Kobayashi has a fondness for ballet, especially Anastasia Kuznetsov. Mention her and he will definitely invite you to the private game. She recently broke her Anterior Tibiofibular"

"I travelled into Azurite City for work, a famous ballerina," I clicked my hand as if I was trying to recall the name "Kuznetsov, um..."

Kobayashi interrupted and took the bait "Anastasia!"

"Yes, that's her name. Yes, Anastasia needed a surgeon, her career was in jeopardy. Her Anterior Tibiofibular, If I recall"

"She is an incredible dancer, the best in the world" Kobayashi's eyes were alight with glee, the thought of her excited him, made him almost tremble.

"The finest surgeon in all of Cadmium City, I assure you. He saved her, and I saw the way he treated her, a true gentleman" Zhou added,

"Come, I must hear more, Join me" Kobayashi gestured for me to follow. I was in, just like that. I thought it might have taken some time, a little more schmoozing of a few more guests.

"You go, I have a few guests and some juicy gossip to catch up on" Zhou bowed her head.

Kobayashi waved over to the guards, he had his hand on my shoulder, like a giddy teenager, his excitement got the better of him, and he giggled like a girl. We climbed the stairs which led to the upper floor, gold statues of little tiger cubs stood proud as they guarded the door to the upper floor rooms, emerald green walls adorned with thousands of photos all with Kobayashi shaking hands with powerful figures, politicians, actors, lawyers and surgeons. We continued walking through the corridors on the upper floor, the whole time Kobayashi was unnervingly quiet, a contrast to his giddy act before. Another hulking guard stood, blocking the door, as he shifted aside the lettering on the door became visible. *'Mr Kobayashi'*

"Thank you, I will not be needing your services anymore, please wait outside" the door closed behind us, Kobayashi motioned for me to sit on a couch.

"Can I offer you a drink"

"That would be great, Thanks"

"Now, Mr Moretti, tell me more"

"Well, I don't really know where to start. It was a normal operation, I fixed her fractured Anterior Tib" Kobayashi held his hand up, his palm facing me "Stop!" his face was cross, he had a sour and aggravated look, his teeth clenched, he paced around the room.

"What happened?" I played dumb

"Don't play games with me, You have an amazing story, tell me more about it, from the beginning." Kobayashi's mood changed, a slight smile,

"Ok, Anastasia's agent contacted my office," I continued the ruse, making up details to fluff the story, the whole time Kobayashi placed cards face down on the table. "I arrived at the Maya Theatre and Anastasia was hurt, she was in alot of pain, She had no idea what to do, the show was that night," The deck was black, silver floral designs that shimmered under the right light and angle.

"So what did you do, what happened" Kobayashi asked, placing the last card on the table

"I examined her ankle, the swelling was bad, she had a broken bone, she couldn't perform. An ancient spell called the helande sanitatem was performed, with some root powder and a spritz of alcohol It healed the wound and returned her to perfect condition. It was like a miracle. A power I've always had, but never understood until then. It was amazing, a gift from above." I looked down and saw a deck of cards, laid out in a neat line, face down.

"The healing spell is an ancient technique, not many know of its powers. You must teach me" Mr Kobayashi seemed more and more interested by the minute.

"Sure, if you'd like"

"First, would you join me in a game, Mr Moretti"

"I don't know how to play, but, I'd love to"

"Place your hand over the first card, close your eyes and think of a number, don't tell me" I placed my hand, hovering over the first card. I was a little apprehensive, this was more like a magic trick than a game, but I played along.

"Fantastic!" Kobayashi seemed pleased, he flipped the card and It revealed the number nine.

"This game is easy, you've already won." Mr Kobayashi stared into my eyes, he leaned onto the table, his full weight off his chair.

"I thought you said you'd teach me?"

"Of course, now, do the same with the second card, place your hand over it and close your eyes. This time think of a shape, any shape."

I did as instructed, I closed my eyes and thought of a triangle, a red triangle.

"Amazing!" Kobayashi was pleased, and he flipped the card, A picture of a red triangle.

My body began to feel heavy, like I was sinking into my chair, my limbs started to lose feeling, the cold numbness appeared in my fingertips and slowly crept to my hands, my arms and moved from my toes to my legs. My chest was tight, I could barely breathe.

"W...wha.t's h..hap...pening" I managed to utter

"Mr Moretti, you're dying. Poison. Your brain is shutting down"

"Poison" I gasped.

"Don't worry, It won't last long"

My vision began to blur, I saw two Kobayashis, his voice sounded distant.

"The next card, Mr Moretti, please concentrate"

"C...ard" I stuttered.

"Place your hand over it"

I raised my arm, I could barely see the table in front of me.

"Good, close your eyes, and think of your favourite place"

Thoughts of our little spot on the creek came flooding back, the treehouse, Milo splashing in the shallow water and Natasha playing her guitar, singing her songs

'In this nightmare of my own making, I must find the strength in my waking. To banish the darkness, to break free, And find peace in reality.'

"I know who you are, Mr Moretti, You're not a doctor, you're working for Madame Zhou, why are you here?" Kobayashi's voice bellowed from the skies, I was deep in his trace, a victim to his power. I had fallen for his card game roose and now a lost soul in his grasp.

"C...ard"

"Your hand, please, the card"

I could hear him, his voice was closer, his office table was in the treehouse, in the centre of the room, out of place. My head was light, the pain had subsided. I could feel the poison in my veins, it burned like acid. My body felt cold but I was sweating, a tingling sensation.

I placed my hand over the last card, I had no choice. Kobayashi was in total control. "Good, now, concentrate" His voice was clearer, louder. "Why are you here? Why are you working with Zhou?" He flipped the card, it was an image of the Shíjiān Warrior's book, the image of a serpent squeezing the life out of a scorpion confirmed the book.

"Interesting, she sent you to do her dirty work"

The creek faded to black, the trees dissolved into dust as my senses became clear. My eyes opened and I sat in a chair opposite Kobayashi in his office. He sat back comfortable, he knew everything and basked in the glory of having the upper hand.

"It's ok, you want the book," Kobayashi paused. "It's yours!" The book sat on the desk in front of me, "Do you even know what it does?" he continued

"It's the history and culture of the Shíjiān Warriors, it holds their power, a life force" My energy slowly gained strength, I was unsure of his intentions.

"It does a little more than that, take a look inside, the page is marked"

"No! I'm not stupid, it's a trap, you're trying to trick me"

"I assure you, Mr. Moretti, I'm not tricking you...look" he picked up the book and opened the page, it was the picture of the serpent squeezing the scorpion.

"It's a beautiful painting, why are you showing it to me?"

"Who is the serpent and who is the scorpion?" Kobayashi closed the book, "Let me guess, she wanted you to place it on the pedestal in their library?"

"Devious bitch!" Kobayashi slammed his fist on the desk, the whole room shook,

"It is not a simple task, the pedestal is protected by an array of spells, curses and traps. One wrong move and it will trigger, and destroy the one who holds it, she played you, my friend"

"No, no, no, no. She wouldn't"

"She's been planning this for a while, the rise of the Shíjiān Warriors, our fall from grace. She knew she couldn't resurrect them without this book, without the leader of the warriors, so she found you"

"Me" Yichén's voice interrupted the conversation, Kobayashi froze in place,

Yichén sounded solemn, disappointed and heartbroken. "She fooled us both, Sebastian, I am their leader, the warrior she seeks. with me in spirit form, you can wake the Shíjiān Warriors, offer your life as forfeit, she gains control, gains command of an invincible force." The room lit up, Kobayashi continued "She found Yichén, or at least his spirit" Kobayashi looked angry and vengeful, "Don't fall into her trap, help me eliminate her and I will aid your mission, you will have the Shíjiān Warriors and my shieldmaidens. They will fight together as one, as they did before Zhou"

I sat back, overwhelmed, I was speechless. A simple man living a simple life, now potentially a leader of two armies, caught in deception and murder plotting, I just needed to find Natasha and make sure she was safe. The only way I could guarantee it was with help. Kobayashi's offer was too good to pass, I agreed, and we began to form a plan.

"I will arrange transport for the book, it will be in the library ready for you to place on the pedestal, Take this," Kobayashi handed me a blade, slightly larger than a dagger but not large enough to be a sword, the carving on the hilt depicted a mother cradling her baby, specks of rust formed over the protrusions. The hilt felt cold, even when gripped over time, the magical incantations had strong properties. "Thank you Mr Kobayashi, you had every chance to kill me yet, you helped me. Why?"

"We are not allies, we will never be. Zhou has taken much from us, we both seek revenge"

"Then we have a common goal"

"Indeed, Mr. Moretti"

A knock at the door broke our attention,

"Mr Kobayashi, guests are moving towards the ballroom, the dance is about to begin"

"Thank you," Kobayashi bowed to his assistant. I had got it all wrong. Kobayashi was a good man, a decent man. It was Zhou that was evil and she needed to be stopped. Kobayashi stood up and adjusted his tie,

"You leave first, casually, I'll follow"

"Yes"

The ballroom was silent, the guests moved aside, giving a path for me to walk, I entered the ballroom on the east, Madame Zhou entered on the west. The ballroom was enormous, wooden herringbone tiles went on for what seemed miles, Draped curtains neatly tied into even pleats. The room lit with candles that ran across the entire space on little gold plates that were fixed to the walls. The gentle sound of the violins kicked off the event, with Women on one side and men on the other, they waited for Zhou and I to start. I gracefully played with her fingers before bending to one knee, with a kiss I had the whole room gasp in romance. Zhou placed her hands on my shoulders as I placed mine on her waist, with a slow sway the room ignited and joined us in dance.

"So, is the job done?" Madame Zhou was eager, her attention fully on the mission.

I lied "Smooth as silk, the book is in a safe location" We swayed and glided across the dancefloor, covering the entire room, spinning in unison with the guests around us, I preferred a bottled beer in a midtown bar, singing and stomping my feet to an old country song about trucks, girls in jean shorts and sipping whisky neat from the bottle, but I became what I needed to be, played the part I needed to play.

"Fantastic! let us enjoy the night, like young lovers" The lust in her eyes was clear as day, she had an insatiable appetite for power and would do anything to get it.

"I'd like nothing more" My lies were convincing, Zhou was none the wiser.

The music ended and we stood still, the crowd clapped, we bowed. The violins kicked back in, a softer tempo.

"I need to freshen up" Zhou smiled, she had her hand on my shoulder, "Will you accompany me?"

"It would be my pleasure"

Madame Zhou led the way, the guests bowed and parted as we walked towards the east wing. Zhou was silent, a smile of pure satisfaction on her face. She seemed happy.

We entered the bedroom and the doors closed behind us, a loud bang followed by the click of a lock, Madame Zhou was in a trance, she had the look of lust, of desire, she stared at me like a lion stares at a wounded gazelle, she bit her lip lasciviously as she moved her dress strap off her right shoulder, her red silk dress slid gently over her skin. The light from the moon and the candles danced over her body, she stood in front of the bed, her breasts were pert and her nipples were hard, her hands moved down her curves, she teased, a devilish grin on her face.

"Undress, my sweet," her voice was soft, inviting.

"Yes, ma'am"

She lay back on the bed, and watched me undress, I began to remove my jacket, placing it over the chair. Her eyes followed, a hungry look on her face. Naked, I climbed on top of her, and we began to kiss, a soft, gentle, loving kiss. My hands explored her body, a moan escaped her lips.

"Fuck me, Sebastian, fuck me now" Her nails dug deep into my back, I winced at the pain, she was in control, and she wanted me.

Kobayashi blade was in its sheath wrapped around my belt, out of reach but thankfully out of sight. My hands held her throat, squeezing her neck, she gasped for air, her eyes widened. She enjoyed the loss of control, her submissive nature came through, she gave herself to me.

"Harder!" She cried,

I squeezed tighter, she gasped, her breathing became more rapid, I picked her body up, we were soaked in sweat, I slammed her back onto the bed, sitting upright. The room started to shake, the candles blew out and the curtains fluttered in the breeze.

"Oh god, yes" she cried out, her back arched, her whole body stiffened, she was on the verge.

I let go of her neck, and grabbed her wrists, pinning them above her head. Her mouth opened wide, her eyes were clenched shut.

"That's it, that's it" She was breathless, her moans became screams, she was in ecstasy.

With a final scream her body spasmed, the orgasm took control.

"Wow, wow" Her chest heaved up and down, she tried to catch her breath.

Her eyes were fixed on the ceiling, a smile of pure pleasure was on her face. Her arms lay at her sides, the room was quiet.

"Did you like that, Madame?" I asked.

"Hmm, I'm in heaven, my dear, in heaven" she replied. We lay under the covers and gazed at the glass roof, the stars twinkled above.

"We will rule this world, you and I" Zhou was confident, her voice full of excitement.

"And no one will stop us" Lying became easy, just words I needed to say to carry out the mission, nothing more.

"My love, I have something for you, a gift" Zhou climbed out of the bed, her naked body looked beautiful, her ass was firm, her hips curvy, she was the ideal woman.

She reached down and pulled out a long box, black, with silver edges.

"This is Yichén's Bow, a bow of immense power. When arrows strike a victim, a spell is activated. A curse will cause the victim to suffer unimaginable pain and agony, their last breath will be a cry of horror. Take it, you have earned it"

I was surprised, she trusted me, "Thank you,"

She climbed back into bed and cuddled me, wrapping her leg and arms around my body, like a python strangling its prey.

"Tomorrow will be a day filled with victory, for both of us" Madame Zhou fell asleep, exhausted.

I lay awake, thoughts ran wild in my mind, the mission, the plan, Natasha. My heart sank, I missed her, I was mainly surprised, surprised at the lack of guilt I felt, I just had sex with another woman whilst Natasha was held captive, god only knows what she was forced to endure. I'm here, living it up and nothing, no guilt nor remorse.

The sun rose and I woke up, Madame Zhou was In the shower, she sang softly.

"Sebastian, darling, you want to join me?" Her voice was soft and gentle.

"Of course, give me a minute"

I untied Kobayashi's blade and gripped the hilt tight, I was ready.

I slowly approached the shower. Zhou was standing with her back facing me, water trickling down her naked body.

"Sebastian, I'm ready," her eyes were closed.

I raised the dagger and pointed the tip at her. Zhou turned around and looked directly at me.

"You really thought I was so stupid" She laughed, the laugh was mocking, an insult, "You think I don't have contingencies," She pointed to a small red light under her skin just below her ear lobe, tucked out of sight.

"What is that?" I was confused.

"That, my dear, is a tracker, if my heart rate stops, my men will kill your team, no questions asked" She continued to laugh "You thought I'd trust you with my life, a complete stranger?"

Her laughing fuelled my rage, my vision became clouded, red and white spots flashed in and out.

"You fucking bitch, you won't win!" I held my gaze, we were face to face, my nose touching hers, I watched the life fade from her body, her skin turning pale and her eyes rolled backwards.

"Yichén would have done the same" she whispered as she slowly slid down the white bathroom tiles, blood poured and swirled down the drain, the smell of iron and copper filled the air. The loud silence, like the feeling after a rock concert, it engulfed my senses. The come down after a surge of adrenaline was powerful, the room span and the ground moved, a sudden feeling of emptiness and loss hit me. The red light behind her ear slowly fell dim as it turned off. Not two minutes had passed, three loud bangs woke me from my trance, gunfire from street level over the road. That's when I knew, she wasn't bluffing, my team was gone.

An Ungodly Creature

A Rabid Beast

A being of chaos, of malevolent intent,
It revels in causing misery, leaving hearts rent.
Unholy deeds, it's only pleasure it seems,
A nightmare incarnate, of evil extremes.

The cries of the innocent, fall on deaf ears,
As the ungodly creature feeds on their fears.
A blight on the world, a curse in disguise,
Its presence is a stain, a darkness that never dies.

Beware the whispers in the night,
For the ungodly creature preys on our light.
Stay vigilant, stay strong, do not falter,
For the ungodly creature's grip grows ever darker.

Natasha screamed in agony, her body deformed into a monstrous, grotesque abomination. No longer in control but a passenger to destruction.. Her hands stretched forward and the flames erupted from her gaping mouth, her wings splayed out strong and proudly, The immense heat, scorching as the flames erupted, fiery embers igniting and dancing in the soft breeze. A nagging feeling scratched on the back of her mind, like a splinter, just out of reach, the bloodlust was unquenchable.

The flames spread through the forest, a wildfire that would burn for days.

"Find your prince," Pazandir Commanded, his deep raspy voice bellowing through the trees.

In her new form, her eyes could see the beating hearts of innocent victims, she found them to be a mockery of her former life, the demon's spell allowed her to see the souls of the living, like flickering lights in the darkest of nights. In her mind she could see Sebastian's soul, her heart skipped a beat, her breath caught in her throat.

"Yes, master," Natasha unwillingly replied.

Her wings flapped harder and faster, and her strength and speed increased. The fire and heat she felt within was incredible, a feeling of pure power surged through her. Her body moved as if it were a well-oiled machine, a deadly assassin on a mission to kill her prince and bring him to her master.

Peridot City was the closest settlement to Pazandir's lair, brought to rubble and ash the flames engulfed the city, the people fled, but so few survived. Their bodies were mutilated and charred, a mass slaughter.

Natasha searched for Sebastian's soul, the bright light shining from afar, guiding her to her target. As she flew above the city, the overwhelming thirst for violence was irresistible. Natasha swooped down like an eagle hunting its prey, silent and deadly, her eyes fixated on the target. Some of the citizens had returned to the city, adamant to build and repair their homes, a grave mistake. Landing softly she placed her clawed feet on the dirty, rubbled road. With each step, Natasha sniffed out the sweet scent of life, a similar smell to roast chicken, the crackling of pork and the juicy tenderness of succulent meat. Natasha's eyes grew large and darted back and forth, scanning the street for her prey, her wings flared out to their full length, muscles flexing as she readied for an attack.

A Knight stepped out from behind a large boulder, the remnants of a tall building that had fallen, dust, dirt and debris covered the area in a thick layer. She carried a sword in her right hand and a shield in her left, strapped to her forearm, she held it tight to her chest, the emblem of the Dark Watch. The brave Knight dawned leather armour, scratched and battered, it endured a lifetime of war and saw many foes fall, it was covered in ash and soot, her

187

face hidden behind a black scarf, presumably to keep her airways clear. She watched Natasha from a distance, her heart racing, sweat pouring down her brow. She was a Knight, trained in combat and tactics, she had fought demons before, but not like this. The knight stepped out into the open, her sword drawn and ready, her shield raised, tall and rectangular covering her entire body.

"Beast, show yourself," she demanded.

Brave and strong, and very determined. The knight had seen her city burn and her people slaughtered. She had not given up hope, but she was angry, her face burned red with rage, her eyes filled with tears, her hands and arms shaking, not from fear, but from sheer uncontrollable anger.

Natasha stepped towards her, her claws clicking on the cobblestone streets, the sound reverberated off the walls, bouncing around in the knight's head, she could feel her heartbeat quicken, her throat tighten. She could sense her fear, her soul shimmered and quivered, a bright green, like fresh leaves. She could almost taste the fear in the air, the scent was intoxicating, sweet and rich.

"Show yourself, monster, in the name of the Dark Watch, I, Lt Gen Anna Isaac will have you meet me in battle! " the knight yelled.

The brave Knight stood firm, her feet planted on the ground, her sword steady in her hand, that's when the beast fully emerged. Natasha stood tall at the end of the street, the distance was far enough for safety but close enough that danger was imminent. A thing of beauty, a four-legged beast that could fly, her wings stretched out wide, her muscles rippling and bulging, scales covering her body and shone brightly. The knight stood in awe, mesmerised by the creature, her beauty, her strength, she dropped her shield, her sword fell to the floor, her knees buckled as she dropped to the ground.

Natasha took the opportunity, and she lunged forward, her speed and agility were impressive, she leapt across the street and landed directly in front of the knight. She stared at her, her eyes filled with fear, her heart raced, her breathing erratic. The Knight's throat was tight and dry from the ash in the air, words failed to form under the immense stress. Natasha brought her head down to her face, her snout barely an inch away, her teeth dripped with blood from her fresh kill, her fangs glistened in the sunlight.

"Please, no," the knight whimpered.

She held up her hands, her palms out in defence, her fingers curled into fists. She wanted to fight, but the beast was too strong, the fear and panic had overtaken her body. Natasha took advantage, she could smell the Knight's fear, the sweat on her forehead, the rapid pulse in her neck. Natasha slowly opened her mouth and took in a deep breath, her lungs expanding and her chest puffed out. She held her breath, a long drawn out breath, she savoured the smell, the taste, the feeling. Natasha closed her eyes, a smile creeping across her face.

Natasha released the air slowly, her exhale lasted longer than the inhale, Natasha's body relaxed, her shoulders dropping as her wings folded neatly behind her. Natasha opened her eyes, her pupils were dilated, her irises a deep blue, a soft calming blue, her eyes focused on the knight, her mind clear and her heart calm.

"Please, spare me," the knight begged, her voice was weak

Natasha let out a long soft growl, not a growl of intimidation or that from an animal in fear, no, it was a purr, a gentle, kind, warm and inviting purr.

"I'll take my time with you, enjoy every moment"

Natasha's tongue slid out from between her teeth, her eyes fixed on the knight's neck, the vein throbbing. Her mouth salivated, her tongue ran over her fangs, the taste of fresh blood sent a rush through her body, her heart rate increased sending her breathing quick and shallow. Natasha reached forward, her claws wrapped around the knight's neck, squeezing tight, cutting off her airway.

"Please," the knight pleaded, her voice a faint whisper.

The smell of sweat, the taste of salty fear, Natasha was overcome by the delicious scent, the temptation too great. Her mind was lost, her senses taken over, and her instincts kicked in. She licked her lips and bit down hard on the knight's neck. The pain was overbearing, a searing hot stabbing pain, a white hot flash that shot through her body, sending her into convulsions. The knight's screams were muffled by the weight of Natasha's claws.

Natasha was lost in the moment, her heart was racing. Natasha felt an intense power surge from the knight into her body, she grew stronger and faster, her claws tightened their grip, the knight's face turning a shade of blue. Natasha opened her mouth wide and let out a scream, a guttural roar, a call to the heavens that rumbled the earth and woke the deepest pits of hell. The knight's eyes rolled into the back of her head, her body fell limp, her heart stopped, life had left her.

Natasha dismembered the corpse, she gorged herself on the knight's flesh, her hunger insatiable, her thirst unquenchable. Blood and bone splattered across the street, the gore was immense, a feast fit for a queen, or in this case, an insatiable beast.

With her belly full, her thirst sated, her lust for flesh fulfilled, Natasha set her eyes on her target. A deep crevasse formed around her feet, cracks, metres wide unearthed the cobble street. Her wings unfolded, her back arched, her head tilted towards the sky. Flames erupted from her mouth, the heat and power of her breath melting the rock and dirt around her. She roared a loud roar that shook the foundations of the world, the sound of her voice, the fury of her heart, the wrath of her soul, her love, her life, her will.

A fiery glow emerged from the depths, it lit the street of ash and dust. Creatures of shadow and horror climbed and clambered over each other to the surface, they lowered their heads and bowed in honour and praise. They had been awakened by the call.

"To war, my minions, we will conquer and destroy," Natasha screamed.

Her voice boomed with power and authority, her army gathered and marched behind her, a legion of creatures, nightmares and terrors. She marched north to Saint Morgan in search of her love and destroyed everything in her path.

"Sebastian, my love, I'm coming for you," the beast said, a cruel smile spread across her face.

The wind whistled and the sky grew dark, a storm brewed, clouds gathered and rains fell.

"My children, march with me, your mistress, your mother, we will march across the world and claim our birthright, the destruction of humanity, in the name of Pazandir!"

The army marched on, a legion of monsters and demons, a swarm of death and destruction, Pazandir's plague upon mankind.

The Hero must fall for a Villian to rise

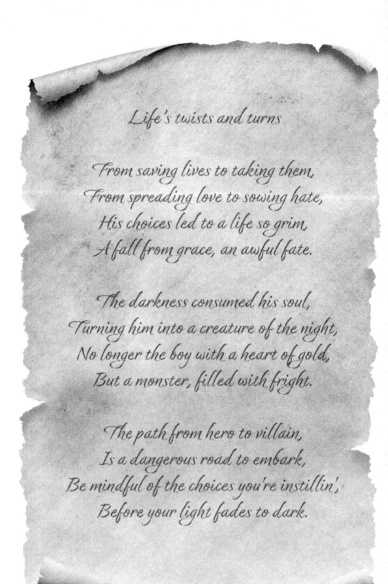

Life's twists and turns

From saving lives to taking them,
From spreading love to sowing hate,
His choices led to a life so grim,
A fall from grace, an awful fate.

The darkness consumed his soul,
Turning him into a creature of the night,
No longer the boy with a heart of gold,
But a monster, filled with fright.

The path from hero to villain,
Is a dangerous road to embark,
Be mindful of the choices you're instillin',
Before your light fades to dark.

I fell to my knees, guilt-ridden and distraught. How could I have just sacrificed my team like that? My friends. At the drop of a hat, the slightest, smallest promise of power beyond my wildest dreams and I falter. A stranger's promise with no guarantee. Zhou's body lay in the shower, the wound poured with blood as it swirled down the drain, her life faded away. The water still ran, trickling over her perfect, lifeless body.

I stepped back, what had I become, a monster, thirsty for blood, capable of horrific acts, in the name and pursuit of power. I could feel her gaze on me, her body lying there judging the acts I committed, I needed out. I dashed for the exit, leaving the bathroom door open, the noise of the running water was all I heard as I flew across the room, a constant, steady noise, everything else fell silent. I had nothing left, nothing. I was alone. Betraying my team, Betraying Natasha, Betraying myself.

Flingling my shirt and trousers on I made for the east wing, the corridors were empty. In the early hours of the morning, I guess the other guests were either asleep or had woken abruptly by the gunfire. The sound of my feet as I walked at a panicked pace echoed.

A group of Kobayashi's guards approached me, four bulky men in matching black and navy suits, the monochrome attire was surreal, formal without the fashion flair or splash of colour, they blended in perfectly, however, the blacked out wrap-around shades and coiled earpiece cable made it obvious who they were.

"We're here to take her body," the guard was emotionless, his voice flat. News must've travelled about my 'successful' mission, I hated myself, hated what I had become, hated that I enjoyed Zhou's company and forgot all about Natasha.

"She's in the shower, make sure to be respectful"

"Yes sir," the guard bowed, and continued on his way,

The front door was open, the sun shone through the gap, the cool air rushed in and filled the space. Everything moved so fast, I ran on instinct and impulse, the moments flashed like a blur.

"Sir, your ride is here" A man stood in the doorway, he wore a grey suit, the buttons strained to keep his belly in, a white shirt and a thin black tie, his hair was combed back, his thick moustache curled at the edges. I looked past his shoulder at the team Humvee, Kobayashi's men carried bodies from the back seats into a white van and hurled ass around the corner, the tyres screeched and left tracks on the road, the sound felt like a sharp stabbing pain in my chest, My heart sank, I had failed, I had failed them.

"Where is Kobayashi?" My voice was stern.

"Mr. Kobayashi has left, He apologises for the lack of courtesy but he will meet you at the Shíjiān Library" The driver replied as he followed the white van, racing through the narrow streets, perfectly dodging obstacles and timing traffic lights for the swiftest journey back, I got the feeling they wanted to avoid being seen at the crime scene, being tied to Zhou's death.

I sat in silence as the city rolled past, the buildings towered over me, like bent over trees, watching, judging. The streets were awakening, even in the early hour of the morning the locals were active, slinging black plastic bags into trash cans, grabbing the local newspaper from the doorstep. The humidity was high and the air was thick, the back of my shirt stuck to the leather seat.

"Sir, we have arrived" The car stopped, and the engine cut off. "Mr Kobayashi is waiting...the library"

"Thank you" I bowed slightly, and he returned the gesture. Stepping out of the car and onto the street felt unnerving, like someone was about to approach me and question my decisions, I felt naked, naked and ashamed. I should have just disappeared, left the city and looked for Natasha myself, I was compelled to see the mission to the end, my thoughts were focused on the end goal. Power.

The Shíjiān Library was located on the basement level of the building, I approached the front steps, but the lack of security took me back, the two hulking goliaths were gone, the swivel door stood empty and open, the lights from the foyer beamed out onto the street, nobody was home. I tread carefully up the stairs, I fully expected an ambush, I was in luck, as I made my way across the foyer and down the stairs thoughts raced around my mind. What if Kobayashi was bluffing? Saying what I wanted to hear, luring me into a false sense of security. I had no way of confirming whether I was right or wrong, second-guessing my action could never turn back time, I had to move forward, assuming everything was to plan. The door leading to the library at the bottom of the stairs was open. The place was empty. The walls climbed forever, an impressive feat for a basement library, made from black marble, swirls of white and grey danced and carved patterns into the solid cold wall. Rich dark wooden structures held ancient books, the room had a stale, dusty, damp smell.

"Kobayashi!" I shouted.

The echo was all that greeted me, reverberations of my own voice, like my inner monologue chatting to myself. I moved slowly and cautiously, my mind racing and my senses on high alert.

"Hello Sebastian" A deep, gruff voice from the shadows spoke, the sound startled me, and the hairs on the back of my neck stood.

"Mr Kobayashi, a pleasure"

"No need for formalities"

"Where is the book, Mr. Kobayashi, did you find it?"

"Yes, it is here"

Kobayashi handed me the book, he opened it and left it on the correct page. Kobayashi led the way to the pedestal, he knew his way around which surprised me. In the centre of the room was a clearing, a space no larger than a couple of metres squared, surrounded by ornate statues of warriors, all dressed in garments from different periods in time. The figures stood tall and proud, I was in awe, the detailing and craftsmanship were inspiring. The closest one was dressed in hide and fur, ruffles of feathers span from his head as he gazed up and grasped his spear tight, muscles bulged from every limb, an impressive sight. One by one I studied as they advanced in technology and armour, from furs and leather to bronze and iron, chainmail and metal plates, then finally formal attire wielding magic and mystical items, wands and staves, combined with guns of all types.

"Are you ready?" Kobayashi asked.

"Yes, I am" I was confident, surprised really, considering the events just passed, the allure of power clouded my judgement, and made me reckless.

"This ritual will take a great deal of energy, you will be able to perform this one time and one time only, so make it count"

"Yes, Sir"

"Let's begin,"

I placed my finger on the page and began to read the spell carefully,

'Into the unknown with courage and might, Embrace the power you hold within, To shape your future, to create your fate, No force can stand in your way, no storm, Can shake your resolve or break your form, Rise great army of warriors, come and hear my command, Prepare yourselves for battle, for we must stand strong, The enemy approaches, we must fight for our land, With courage in our hearts, we will not be wrong. Shoulder to shoulder, we will fight side by side, Honor and glory, in victory we shall bide.'

The room began to shudder and shake, books fell from their shelves, dust and plaster rained from the ceiling. The statues began to move, each warrior stepped off its pedestal and joined me in the middle.

"What the hell is going on"

Kobayashi didn't speak, he watched in awe, the look of terror in his eyes, he had never seen such power, never seen the Shíjiān army in their glory.

One by one, the statues began to take shape, a shimmering aura engulfed their forms, the warriors began to take on human appearance, real flesh and bone. They were alive, a living breathing army, thousands of years of warriors and fighting techniques, all under my command.

"We await your orders, master" A large, muscular, Japanese man approached me, his arms were bare, showing off his bulging muscles, his long hair tied up in a ponytail. His armour was black and made of leather, his hands covered in black, fingerless gloves. His voice was familiar.

"Yichén?"

"It's been a while, Sebastian" Yichén was calm and relaxed, he had a proud smile, I was worried he knew about Zhou.

"How are you, here?"

"This is the power of the Shíjiān Ritual, the power to control time and space, to command the ancient warriors of Shíjiān"

Kobayashi interrupted "As promised, you have eliminated the Shíjiān clan from Azurite City and claimed the army for yourself, this leaves my people free to thrive without danger of warring over territory" He bowed and handed me a necklace, the necklace matched the design of the blade, ornate and delicate, made of gold and precious gems. I bowed and took the necklace, the weight was surprising and heavy, a burden to hold in my hand, I raised it and placed it slowly over my head, the anticipation was exciting and nerve-wracking, I had no idea what was about to happen. Mr Kobayashi smiled, the pendant glowed as it sat in the middle of my chest, warm and comforting it felt right, familiar.

"They await, outside" Kobayashi bowed and left the room, leaving me and Yichén to ourselves.

"You have been a great asset, Sebastian"

"And you, Yichén"

"We will see each other again soon" Yichén disappeared, and the warriors disappeared with him, I was alone in the room to reflect on the accomplishments I had achieved, not a thought about the betrayal it took.

I left the library and walked up to the building's exit, clutching the necklace pendant and admiring the gem's glow. I glanced up to the street below and dropped the pendent, it swung from my neck as I stood Gob-smacked and shocked. A horde of shield maidens stood at attention and waited for my command. The Amazonian warriors stood proud and strong, each one a sight of beauty, all dressed in their finest armoury, scantily clad, wielding spears, axes and bows.

"Master, what is your command?" the lead shield maiden spoke.

"I..." I had no words, the sight was beyond anything I could ever imagine. Yichén appeared behind me, placing his hand on my shoulder, and imbuing me with his strength.

"We stand on the dawn of hope, a beast of shadow and bone seeks to destroy this land, destroy our people and destroy all that is good. We stand an army of warriors, warriors of magic, might and valour, the time has come to stand against evil and restore balance to this world. It is our duty, and destiny, to stand and fight for the greater good. Evil lurks in the dark, waiting and watching, it seeks to claim and conquer, destroy and decimate, the enemy will rise and gain power, the time is now. We will not wait, we will strike, and we will end the darkness."

A roar of cheer and applause rang from the women, the energy and excitement were intoxicating, my adrenaline pumped, and my heart raced.

"We march south, to Pazandir's lair, to victory....to WAR!"

Cheers echoed and the shield maidens cheered, Yichén turned and gave me a reassuring nod. I led the charge, the army moved swiftly behind me, marching with purpose and determination, the energy and atmosphere were contagious, a feeling I had never felt before, I had control, power and strength, this was my time, this was my moment.

We moved along the empty streets, the sun beating down at its highest point in the sky, the rhythmic stomp of armoured boots pounded the road and made my chest throb, a constant pounding. We reached the city exit and were met by a swarm of the undead, hundreds, thousands.

"The first line of defence" Yichén spoke,

"What are these abominations?" I was confused, the dead could not walk. Or so I thought.

"Yes, these are the risen, the dead reborn by an evil, dark magic. Birthed from the depths of hell, they have climbed through fire and lava to surface"

"How do we stop them?"

"You command the warriors, you have the power, they are weak and mindless, a distraction. We move forward, and strike Pazandir"

"Let us charge and defeat this distraction...CHARGE!"

A deafening war cry was heard, the shield maidens and the warriors surged forward, their weapons ready and their bodies eager for battle. The undead horde charged the first wave met and clashed, a sea of bodies and blood filled the field, the dead and dying. The smell of blood and ash choked the oxygen from the area, the thick, hot smoke billowed and covered the battleground. That's when I saw her, saw the beast that became her.

Her body was half-dragon, a quadruped, her soft sensual skin had hardened into scales of armour, red and vibrant to ward off enemies, half woman, her face still recognisable, instead of a sweet innocent smile, a bloodlust scowl, searching for her next victim. Her wings stretched out and flapped as she spotted me on the other side of the river.

"My love, we have found each other, let us be one again, let us embrace" Natasha's voice was raspy and deep,

"Natasha? Is that really you?" I was shocked, hurt, disgusted,

"Yes, my love, it is me. I belong to Pazandir now" Her words cut deep, I had failed her, in more ways than she knew.

"Natasha, please, return to me, to our love, we can escape, live in peace, away from this hell. We can find a cure, a cure to turn you back." I begged and pleaded for her to end this madness. I tried to reach my Natasha, the Natasha I knew,

"I am sorry, Sebastian, but the beast will not allow me to return to the light, to the weak. Not without you" Her clawed hand pointed at me, she wanted me dead.

"I don't want to hurt you, Natasha, but you have forced my hand" I gripped my rifle, my blade holstered for emergencies.

"Then prepare to die" Natasha lunged at me, her massive frame landed a few metres away, the shockwave from her impact knocked me off my feet, she had grown powerful, her new form had given her a surge of strength and energy.

She swiped her massive paw and caught me, the claws tore the flesh on my arm, my blood dripped and mixed with the puddles on the ground. Her teeth glistened in the sun, she snapped and bit down on the air as she closed the gap.

I pulled the sword from its scabbard and readied myself, my wounds caused searing pain, the heat and the humidity were not helping the situation. My breath was heavy, the air was thick, sweat poured from my forehead, the sword weighed heavy in my hand, the pain and strain were beginning to take their toll, and I was tired, exhausted. Natasha circled me, the snarls and growls sent a shiver down my spine, her gaze locked on me, the hunger and rage in her eyes, I knew what had to be done. I had no choice, my love had become a monster, a beast that would not hesitate to kill me.

"I love you, Natasha" I spoke as I readied the blade, a final strike, a fatal blow.

Natasha stopped, she looked at me and her body began to transform. A trick, It was Pazandir testing my will, testing my strength. He was no match for my resolve, I knew my task, my mission. Natasha's features softened, her scales melted away, and her face changed. I have to admit it threw me back a little, seeing Natasha in her beauty again.

"Spare me, spare my life and we can defeat Pazandir, together" Her voice was soft and sweet, innocent. Her eyes still glowed red "Sebastian, wait! What are you doing? Please, don't" Natasha cried, her tears streaming down her cheek.

"I'm sorry, my love"

"Sebastian, no, NO!"

Natasha's cries were too late, the sword pierced her heart, and I drove it into her. I held her close and watched the life fade from her eyes, her body grew cold and lifeless, the tears would not stop, would not ease the pain.

"Natasha, I love you" I whispered into her ear.

Natasha's body began to change, the blood from her body began to boil, steam and vaporise, her corpse started to bubble and pop, her body became a mass of blood and gore. A portal opened, and the blood was drawn to it, the vortex sucked the remains into the black void.

The battle had ended, the abominations had fallen, and the shield maidens and warriors stood in victory. The portal remained open,

"Join me, Sebastian." Pazandir's voice boomed from the vortex.

"What, what is this?" I was confused and startled by the voice from the void

"Join me, Sebastian, Join me in battle to end this, end the terror and bloodshed, you and I."

I looked at Yichén and the shieldmaiden, they nodded and agreed to the proposition. It all felt like a trap, another trick to catch me off guard.

The Eve of Battle, The Great War

War

On the eve of battle, I stand tall and proud
My heart is strong, my head unbowed
I have trained for this moment, for so long
I have pushed myself, to be brave and strong

I have overcome obstacles, both big and small
I have faced my fears, I have stood tall
On the eve of battle, I feel a sense of peace
A calmness within, a sense of release

The night embraces me, a cloak of power,
Guiding me forward, in this darkest hour.
I walk with purpose, my spirit unbroken,
The darkness within, a token.

I approached the shimmering liquid slowly, cautiously. I had my reservations, to just invite me closer to his lair without a plan would be foolish, Pazandir was no fool. The cool gelatinous liquid felt wet to the touch, refreshing and invigorating. My muscles flexed as I stood there, the power, the strength I felt was incredible, it was intoxicating. I let myself sink into the liquid, as I advanced it pulled me more. It crept up my hand and slowly crawled to my elbow. I was nervous the entire time, the battle we had just won could all be for nothing, if I rushed in and sacrificed the higher ground. I pushed forward, there was no point second-guessing myself now, all or nothing. I raised my leg and pushed my foot through, stepping into the void and taking the leap of faith, the rush of adrenaline was euphoric, a feeling unlike any other.

I emerged on a large field, a campsite, but the entire place was empty, tents, firepits and workshops for weapons and armour were all set up and stoked.

"Rest tonight, for tomorrow we fight" Pazandir's voice boomed over the skies, it sounded like it came from the clouds. Yichén and the shield maiden stepped out from the portal with me.

"This feels like a trap" said the Shieldmaiden as she gripped her pike tightly and held her buckler close to her chest.

We walked around, trying to find someone or something, there was not a soul, not a single creature or monster to be seen. We scattered, filling the tents and warming our battle-worn bodies by the fire.

It was cold and the fires were warm, the flames danced as the log beneath glowed, bright and red. Yichén sat down and rested, he had been fighting all day, and the night was a welcome respite. The shieldmaiden took shifts, guarding the single opening to the camp, one way in, one way out, they sat atop a wooden fence post, her eyes peeled and ready.

"Yichén?" I called out, Yichén stood behind me, mingling with the Shíjiān warriors, the laughter and tomfoolery were joyful and full of life. A welcome break from stories of doom and gloom and the end of times.

"Sebastian!" he ran over and clasped my arm in the warrior's handshake, his smile was warm and friendly.

"How have you been, what has been going on since we parted?" He had a large mug of ale in his hand and was eager to chat.

"Back in Azurite City, when," Yichén interrupted with a giant smile on his face

"When I was a mere shadow guide, a presence in your mind?" He raised his eyebrow and smirked, "When you bedded my woman?" He was mocking me.

"Well, I mean, it was more complicated than that, the two of you had a history" Yichén waved his hands at me and brushed it off, "She was a fine woman, beautiful and strong, a perfect match for great warriors like us, and besides, it was only the once" he laughed. "I'm technically dead, she is very cunning and manipulating, you did what you had to. Plus look at us now, in charge of two armies and on the eve of battle."

"Yichén, we have been through a lot" I began, he stopped me mid-sentence, "Sebastian, you are a great friend and brother, I have never had the opportunity to be part of something bigger than myself, you showed me a new life, a new perspective. And now we get to do it again" he took a long sip of his ale, his eyes fixated on the fire in front of us.

"Sebastian, this is a once-in-a-lifetime experience, a chance to end a war, to defeat a great evil and vanquish a demon. The fact that I get to share this experience with you, is a bonus. I'm not just your guide, I am your friend, and you are mine."

I looked over at the Shieldmaiden, their faces stern and stoic, their eyes fixated and alert. I continued with Yichén,

"What's the plan tomorrow?"

"Simple, we kill Pazandir," he said in a matter-of-fact tone, as though it were obvious and clear.

"But how?" I asked

"With the might of an army" Yichén pointed out, gesturing to the rows of tents and sleeping warriors.

"The might of an army, the might of two armies, the might of a million armies" Yichén stood up and shouted, "I know we can win, I have faith in our armies, in our strength and our courage." The ale clearly had an effect on him, "To victory!" he shouted, raising his cup in the air and chugging the last drop.

I stared into the fire, its hypnotic and alluring flames entrancing my gaze. The warmth was comforting, a welcome reprieve from the chill and bitter air. I whispered under my breath "To Victory" and sipped on the last dregs of wine.

I took a walk through the campsite, leaving Yichén to bumble and boast about past victories. The sounds of metal smithing, and leatherworking. The smells of the evening feast wafted through the air. I stopped, the aroma was delicious, my stomach rumbled, and my mouth watered, it had been days since my last meal.

I took a deep breath, the sweet savoury smell of meat and gravy, the hearty broth and the succulent taste. The sound of the sizzling juices, the meaty flavours.

"Hello Sebastian" a woman's voice, soft and delicate

I bowed as I entered the larger tent, rows of warriors sat on benches and filled the space. It was a grand feast, with tables of food and ale, the air was filled with smoke and the sounds of merriment.

"Slow-cooked beef stew in a dark stout with all the trimmings?" she spoke, her words soft and gentle, like a breeze in a field.

"What is your name?" I asked

"Cassandra, my name is Cassandra" She bowed and extended her arm, inviting me to the table.

She was gorgeous, her hair was black as night, her eyes a deep brown, like pools of dark chocolate. Cassandra's soft plump lips were inviting, intoxicating. She had a full voluptuous figure, curvy yet strong and powerful. She moved with a grace and elegance that was unheard of, her poise was immaculate, and her posture perfect.

"Come sit with me," she said as she sat down and gestured to the space next to her.

I took a seat, and a young servant boy placed a large plate in front of me, it was heaped full of the most delectable treats, tender meat and thick juices, the potatoes were brown and crispy, the carrots and peas, all vibrant and nourishing. The meal was exquisite, the best meal I have had in ages, the company was also wonderful.

Cassandra and I spent the evening talking and getting to know one another. She was a shieldmaiden, skilled with a sword and a brilliant leader. We laughed and shared stories. She was a great listener, the way she sat and listened with interest and enthusiasm, her eyes wide and her ears attentive. She would lean forward and nod at the appropriate moments. It was as though she could feel the same things I did, the excitement, the fear, the adrenaline. I felt needed, heard, important and valid. I didn't need to hide who I was or pretend, she wasn't judging, and she was not expecting anything from me. I felt a connection, a deep bond between us, a familiarity and comfortableness.

"Tomorrow will be our greatest battle, our greatest victory" My confidence soared, and my ego was inflated. Cassandra saw right through the bullshit and held my hand, she gazed into my eyes and held her expression, a look of worry and fear, her eyes welled up with tears, and her brow furrowed.

"Tomorrow may be our last day, if we were to fail, the world would be lost"

The night was drawing to a close, the feast was winding down and the festivities were coming to an end. I helped tidy the mess, cleaning plates and clearing the area. The two of us were alone, the rest of the warriors were preparing for bed, sharpening blades, polishing armour and praying.

"Cassandra" I turned around and spoke softly.

"Yes Sebastian?" she replied, I walked closer to her, gently pressing my body against hers and cupping her cheek in my hand, her eyes were wide and full of excitement, her body trembling, her breathing was shallow and quick.

"Cassandra," I said as I leaned forward and kissed her deeply. Our bodies pressed together, her hands ran down my head and gripped the back of my neck tightly. I reached down and lifted her, wrapping her legs around my waist.

I carried her into the tent, our lips locked until she pulled away. She stood at the end of the bed, her body a sight of perfection, her skin smooth and supple, her curves, full and lush. Her breasts heaved and her eyes beckoned me forward. She reached down and grabbed my pants, her hand gently brushing against my cock, sending a shiver down my spine. We were naked, the excitement and adrenaline coursing through our bodies. Cassandra smiled and giggled, she took her scarf and tore it into two, climbing over my body she fastened the knot around my wrists and bound them to the headboard.

"Don't ruin the surprise" she whispered into my ear and kissed my neck. Her lips were soft and gentle, her touch, sensual and alluring. She took the second piece of fabric and tied it over my eyes, she wanted to keep the surprise intact.

"I'll be right back, My prince" She kissed me deeply, her tongue dancing in my mouth. She slowly pulled away, her lips lingering, her breath filling my mouth.

"Don't worry, I will come back" she giggled a devilish laugh that sent shivers down my spine. She was gone and the tent was quiet, I became curious and concerned, what was she planning? I wasn't ready for the surprise she had.

"I'm here," she said in a whisper, her voice was right beside me, I could feel the warmth of her body next to me. I could smell her perfume, a subtle lavender mixed with rose. She untied the scarf around my eyes leaving my hands bound above my head. Three more women entered the tent, all as beautiful as Cassandra, their bodies strong and athletic, their figures curvy and lush. Their bodies were covered in scars, war wounds, stories of victory and loss. They joined us on the bed, their hands caressing my skin, their fingers running up and down my body.

"My prince" Cassandra cooed "we will take care of you, make you feel good on the eve of battle" She ran her tongue over my ear and bit the lobe. The excitement caught my breath as I struggled to focus.

"We'll show you a night like no other" Her breath was hot on my neck, the women were giggling and laughing, their hands touching every inch of my skin, their tongues tasting and exploring.

"Don't worry my prince, just lay back and enjoy the ride" The four women surrounded me, their bodies pressing against me, the warmth and smoothness of their skin, the softness and gentleness of their touch. We exhausted every position, We danced a tango of sex and passion. We made love, hard and fast, soft and gentle. Their screams of pleasure and cries of ecstasy echoed throughout the campsite, the rest of the warriors and armies knew that we were enjoying ourselves.

Cassandra held my body close, her eyes fixed on mine. Her fingers trailed along my cheek and down my chest, her nails tickling my skin and making me giggle. The other three women were asleep, cuddled in a pile of pillows and blankets. Cassandra's eyes were wide and full of wonder, her gaze fixated and her pupils dilated.

"Sebastian, there is something I have to tell you" Her voice was soft and tender, a hint of worry in her tone.

"Yes, Cassandra," I responded. She took a deep breath and let out a sigh.

"There is a prophecy" her words were heavy, and her voice trembled.

"A prophecy, what kind of prophecy?" I asked.

"Pazandir needs to be whole, he seeks his other half, having heard your stories, your journey here. I know, I am certain, he seeks you." she paused, her eyes welling up with tears. "Natasha is not dead, he will remake her, stronger and more grotesque, she will be the key to your demise" She wiped the tears from her eyes and took a deep breath.

"Sebastian, you are the last hope for this world, and you have the potential to save others. You are the only one who can defeat him, the only one who can put an end to his madness, you must defeat him in combat."

"However there will be a cost to your victory," The interruption of soldiers outside the tent rustling and waking after a drunken slumber caused Cassandra to pause. "You will gain his powers, it will either scar you or destroy you" My arrogance laughed her tales of fantasy off.

"Cassandra, you have nothing to worry about, Pazandir is weak, we have a chance to end his terror" I said as I pulled her in close and wrapped my arm around her, her body trembled, and she was cold, her breathing shallow.

"Sebastian, if you were to fall, then we would have no chance, the war is won or lost by you. There is a reason the shield maiden chose you, the reason the spirit guides chose you." I cuddled her tighter "Shhh, calm now, we have a few hours left, let's rest" I cooed. Cassandra took a deep breath and exhaled, she turned to me and smiled.

"You are a great man, a noble warrior, I wish we had more time." she kissed me and laid her head on my chest, the beating of my heart soothed her, the warmth of my body comforted her. We fell asleep in each other's arms.

A Change of Plan

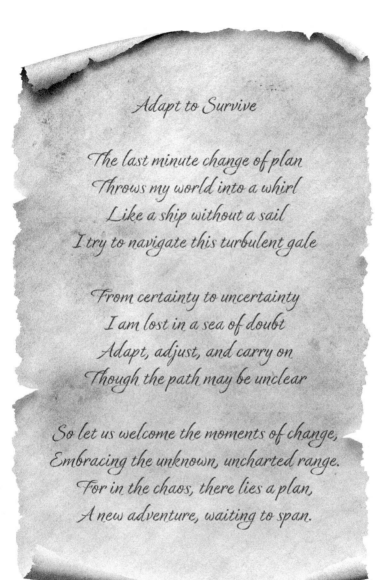

Adapt to Survive

The last minute change of plan
Throws my world into a whirl
Like a ship without a sail
I try to navigate this turbulent gale

From certainty to uncertainty
I am lost in a sea of doubt
Adapt, adjust, and carry on
Though the path may be unclear

So let us welcome the moments of change,
Embracing the unknown, uncharted range.
For in the chaos, there lies a plan,
A new adventure, waiting to span.

"Wake up Sebastian, wake up" I could hear Cassandra's voice in the distance, her tone was frantic, and her words rushed. Beams of sunlight pulsed as the sun rose and fought off the night's clouds, the birds were chirping and the smell of morning coffee and freshly cooked bacon filled the air, the sweet meaty scent danced around my nose.

"Sebastian! Wake up" She shook me violently, my head pounded and my eyes hurt. I struggled to focus, the sounds around me were muffled and distant.

"Cassandra" I tried to speak, but my voice was hoarse and raspy, I indulged in too many drinks, and the hangover was setting in.

"We need to move now!" she shouted, the urgency in her voice was clear, and the tension was thick. I stood up and grabbed my armour, the cloth undergarb fit like a glove and kept me warm and dry, it was made to accommodate all weathers. The leather armour strapped and buckled tight and at three different places, underarm, waist and over the shoulder. The kevlar plate was light and sturdy, it was sawn in well and wrapped around my whole upper body. Light and stealthy, with maximum manoeuvrability.

The tactical boots were solid and firm, metal capped and plated. The black military trousers were from my old uniform, a reminder of where I came from and how far from home I was.

225

"We have a problem," Yichén said as he came running into the tent, his face was stern and his voice was panicked.

"What's the issue?" I asked, my voice still weak and my head pounding, each sound felt like a hammer to the head. Yichén drank more than me but he looked fine, a seasoned drinker I suppose.

"Pazandir is on the move, he knows our location, our plan will not work" The urgency in his voice was evident. "The element of surprise is lost, his army approaches from the south." Yichén's tone was heavy, his words slow and calculated. "The north will not be secure, his army will strike soon, our plans are useless now." He kicked a soldier's helmet on the floor, the hollow clang sent shivers down my spine, my teeth chattered in pain.

"We must move now, Sebastian, we have to fight him head on" he gestured for me to follow him. I looked back at Cassandra, she smiled, her eyes were tired, and her hair was a mess, she flagged her shieldmaiden to help her with her armour, sliding her under armour on as fast as possible.

"Yichén, we are outnumbered, we will not stand a chance, Pazandir has the power of a thousand gods."

Yichén paced around the tent, nervous and frantic. "I know, I heard stories of his incredible might, the strength of his army, terrifying."

"Is it true?" I remembered Cassandra's story, Natasha being alive, the need for a duel, the power we shared. "Are we..." I hesitated, unsure of the validity, hoping they were just rumours and myths "Do we have a connection?"

Yichén stopped pacing, his expression changed, the panic on his face was replaced with a calm and collected demeanour, a stoic and determined look, his eyes stern and his brow furrowed.

"It is true, our fates are intertwined, but there is one difference between us and him" he stepped forward and placed his hand on my shoulder. "He wants power for himself, his desire is to be a god, he thinks he is worthy of divinity, but we know, you and I, that we are not." Yichén was right, a desire for power, a need to be more than mortal, an obsession to be a deity, it wasn't just a flaw, my arrogance hid from the world, I was more like him than I knew.

"But" I began, the words left my mouth before I had the chance to stop myself. "If I do become a god, how do we know that I won't fall to the same fate as Pazandir, will I not seek divinity and godhood" I spoke softly, the words stung, a painful truth, a possibility.

"No," Yichén said confidently, "You will not" he paused. "You will not succumb to the corruption and the greed, the obsession and the desire. You are the one, the prophecy is true, the spirit guides chose you for a reason." Yichén stared into my eyes, fierce and strong, he believed in me wholeheartedly, he saw something most could not.

"I must prepare the armies, meet me in the armoury, I have an idea" he ran out of the tent in a hurry "It's a mad plan, but it just might work!" he yelled as he joined the ruckus.

My rifle was cleaned and prepared by one of the shieldmaiden, oiled and loaded, ready for action, as far from the standard issue handguns the army issued us, no this was a work of art, a tool of destruction. An FN2500 bullpup rifle with dual scope at x2 and x8 telescopic sight capability, gas-operated and fully automatic with zero recoil. A gift I helped myself to from Madame Zhou's personal vault. I fixed Kobayashi's blade to the front like a bayonet, it clicked in perfectly.

I left the tent, the morning sun shone brightly, the cool air complemented the warm rays, the sound of the birds was deafening, the hustle and bustle of the campsite was hectic. I found Cassandra waiting for me at the armoury, she was dressed in her finest battle garb, her armour shined and her sword gleamed. The large bin of handguns behind her was almost empty, the shieldmaidens believed in hand-to-hand combat as a must but carried firearms as a backup. It was better to have one and not need it than to need it and not have one.

Yichén followed behind me, his timing impeccable as per usual. I got the feeling Cassandra made more of our night together than I did. I assumed it was a one-night thing, the passion on the eve of battle sent our emotions all over the place. By this time I had become a monster in my own right, selfish and reckless, not the country boy in love anymore. I wasn't ready for love again, a fraction of my old self.

"We prey on his arrogance, his thirst for your blood, Sebastian" Yichén was fired up, he knew Pazandir, knew of his flaws, knew how to manipulate them to gain the upper hand.

"We will make him attack us directly, he will send his strongest and deadliest, they will break through our defences and attack, their only mission is to capture you alive."

"I don't think he will care if I'm dead or alive, he needs my body and soul." I interrupted.

"He can't kill you, not yet. If you die, his plans are foiled, the prophecy is unfulfilled, You must fight hand-to-hand. He has no choice but to keep you alive." Yichén paused.

"His biggest advantage, his army and his forces. He can crush us with sheer numbers, but if we can take away the threat, then we are in with a fighting chance"

"He can't kill us, not yet, he wants you vulnerable and alone, he'll want to show you his might, to torture you. We can't kill him, you'll bear his curse, become evil" Cassandra interjected, she knew the prophecy well, she knew what was at stake.

"But we can hurt him, if he can feel pain, he is vulnerable," I said, the words coming to me like a bolt of lightning.

"That is the plan," Yichén said smiling. "We meet him on the battlefield, and both armies will brace for war, whilst in the shadow you Sebastian, you will flank him and challenge him to combat, one-on-one"

"He will accept, his arrogance will not allow him to refuse," Cassandra said.

"If we time it right, with Pazandir vanquished, his army will fall, back into the depths from where they came"

The plan was solid, and the odds were stacked against us, a suicide mission. We had the potential to defeat him, the risk of failure was great, the price to pay if we were wrong was death. I had no choice but to put my trust in Yichén, the fate of the world rested on his plan and on my shoulders, the burden was great.

The plan was put into motion, the armies were prepared and the soldiers were ready. The shieldmaidens and the warriors stood proudly, awaiting the signal to march into battle, I stayed behind and plotted the approach,

'Taking the road west leads to Saffire Lake, then southwest through the forest of Sanguinity, and finally into the Valley of Erudition.

I tracked the route with my pencil, making sure the route was both fast and safe. The last thing I wanted was to get lost and end up wandering around.

"The time has come" Yichén entered the tent, his armour glistened and his weapon sharp, his confidence was high, but so was his anxiety.

"I will ride ahead, and meet him head-on, the army will stay behind until I give the signal" his voice was deep and full of authority, the man in charge.

"I will join you shortly, the plan will work, I can feel it," I said as I checked the magazine on my firearm, screwing in the silencer and making final checks to buckles and straps.

"Sebastian" Yichén's tone was low, serious. "If things do not go as planned, If I fall, you are the last line of defence, the fate of the world rests on you" his words were heavy, his gaze intense. "it has been a true honour to serve you, to train you and to see you take on such responsibility" I placed my hand on his shoulder and squeezed, "The honour is mine, ride with valour,"

Yichén smiled, he was proud, he had seen the rise of a soldier, a warrior and a leader. The respect was mutual, the bond unbreakable.

"Good luck, Sebastian"

"May your blade be true, Yichén"

He walked out of the tent, his head high, his stride confident, the shieldmaidens stood proud.

I swung my gun around to my back and holstered my sidearm, the ringing in my head had stopped and the smell of breakfast faded, just the smell of leather polish and the sound of anxious silence, I exited the tent and left the camp, the opposite direction to my armies, alone and isolated, the burden was mine and mine alone.

I headed towards Saffire Lake, the path was straightforward and clear, a route less travelled and far from Pazandir's sight. I ran at a steady pace, taking little breaks. I knew Yichén and Cassandra needed me to face Pazandir as soon as possible. Saffire Lake spanned 14.73 km2 large enough for cover from the battlefield and small enough to cover on foot, the easy path was short and ran around the smaller section, the lake glistened as the rays of sun danced, shimmering against the cool breeze. The path was muddy, and the water was shallow. I waded through and crossed a small bridge, large rocks naturally formed the separation and allowed travellers access in single file. The water was cool, but not cold.

After 3 hours of walking, I circled the lake, the water was deeper and the ground rocky, I followed the shoreline east and reached the forest of Sanguinity.

The woods were vast, dense and thick, the trees towered above and the ground was soft, moss and leaves covered the floor. The canopy was thick and provided cover from the sun. Entering the forest engulfed my senses with smells of pine and eucalyptus, smells you wouldn't find in Saint Morgan, to be honest, it was overpowering and intoxicating. Keeping an eye on the path, the route was long, and the way was dark, it was proving to be difficult, the smells had an effect on my senses, they made me light-headed and a little woozy.

I walked through the forest, the sounds of animals echoed and the ground was wet, the leaves were fresh and the air was moist. The canopy kept the forest cool, even with the sun blazing. With each pounding step, I thought of the raging battle on the other side, how the forces of Shíjiān obliterated the waves of evil and triumphed, I felt uneasy not being there. Thinking back, It never occurred to me how things could have been different, with each choice I made, opened a new path and closed another.

I could have taken a different job, not gone down the military route, not joined the force. I could have stayed with Natasha, kept our relationship alive, fought harder, and tried more. Maybe even save them.

The edge of the forest came quicker than expected, I kept pace and allowed my desire for power to drive me forward, the thought of revenge filled my mind, the images of my family being murdered played over and over in my head, I was consumed by hatred and the need to kill.

"Focus" I spoke out loud, the anger was taking hold, I needed to channel it, and harness my full capability. I was close to the Valley of Erudition, the end of the line. The ground was uneven and the land was rocky, I walked with purpose and kept focused.

I could hear the battlefield up ahead, the forces of Shíjiān and the armies of shadow fought, the clash of steel and the sound of guns filled the air, the ground shook as the enemy was destroyed, the screams of the wounded and the cries of the dying sent a shiver down my spine, the smell of blood and the taste of ash and fire.

The Valleys opening was up ahead, the land was flat and the hills were high, the view was breathtaking, the armies of both sides clashed in a sea of blood, the forces of Shíjiān took heavy losses, the shieldmaidens were dwindling, the warriors were fading, the tide had turned for the worse, they needed me, I needed to hurry. Sharp rocks broke apart leaving a small gap for me to squeeze through, the rocks were cold and damp, the passage was long and tight. The smell of dampness and mudd made the air thick and sickening, I had to slide through to make it to the other side, I could barely move, my armour scraped along the rock and my blade caught each rock.

I pushed my body forward, the weight of the rifle on my back was painful, the metal digging into my back and the strap bruising my chest.

The gap widened allowing me to crawl through, I reached the other side and pulled myself free, the smell was gone, replaced with the stench of war, rotting bodies from both sides slowly decaying in the baking heat. The valley's opening was large, the view of the battlefield was clearer, and the sound was deafening. That's when I saw him, Pazandir himself.

Two become One

A fight to the death

The prophecy whispered in shadows cast,
Foretelling a future that seemed steadfast.
But fate's cruel twist took us by surprise,
Revealing truth in unexpected guise.

The stars aligned, the heavens spoke,
But not in the way we dared to invoke.
What once seemed certain turned to doubt,
As reality twisted and turned about.

I beg for forgiveness, I beg for peace
To be rid of this monster, to find release
But until then, I'll roam alone
A creature of evil, a monster unknown.

He towered over his army, his armour was black and his face was red, great horns protruded from his forehead and coiled upwards, and his scaly skin was rough and jagged, as hard as stone. I expected a figure much like a dragon, going by the tales told. His skin resembled thick calluses, he was scarred all over, evidence of battles, waring and terror. A monster in every sense, he held a wooden staff that was old and crooked, branches weaved around each other and tangled into knots. With each step, the earth shook and trembled under his sheer weight.

He laughed, loud and proud, his arrogance was astounding, his muscles rippled under his armour, his arms were thick and his chest was wide. A terrifying sight, he made my sweat cold as ice, his aura was strong, it made my body tingle and my hands shake, and my legs were weak.

"It's now or never" gearing myself up to muster the strength within, the voice in my head screamed every fibre of my being felt anger and fury, I thought of Natasha and the monster he created, the sound of her voice, distorted and broken, I was the chosen one, the last hope for humanity, the only one that can stand up to him. I want to say it was the hero within that gave me the final push to get the job done. Unfortunately, it wasn't, the lure of ultimate power quenched my thirst, I wanted more "His power will be mine."

Pazandir roared and raised his staff, his army marched forward and attacked the army of Shíjiān, they broke through the lines and killed without mercy, they had no fear and no emotion, puppets to their master.

"Pazandir! End this NOW!" I held my gun in the air and fired off a few rounds to gain his attention, his gaze darted towards me. "FACE ME! COWARD!" I yelled, the fear was gone, the hatred was all-consuming, I had one shot.

His army stopped and turned towards their master, Pazandir looked down at me, a smile across his face.

"So the prophecy was true, the human does have a death wish" he roared.

"FACE ME YOU COWARD! FIGHT ME!" the words left my mouth before I had time to think. He stepped forward and placed his staff on the ground.

"So be it, boy. Your death will be painful and slow." His voice was deep and sinister.

He climbed down from the hill and walked towards me, the sound of his footsteps echoed, his stride was confident and his strut was full of arrogance, the ground shook with each step. The smell of sulphur filled the air, the rotten stench of decay and despair, he basked in the glory of torment.

"Let us play, Down your weapons, let us fight the old way" his words were cold and cruel, a creature who has lived a thousand years and has killed a million innocents, his lust for death was insatiable.

"Let's dance"

The army of Shíjiān had gathered around me and stood ready for battle, Cassandra and Yichén both stood behind me.

"Sebastian! Are you sure about this?" Cassandra spoke, her voice was concerned, the worry in her eyes was clear.

"Yes, there is no other way," I replied, my focus on Pazandir, his eyes bore into my soul, his gaze was intense and his stance powerful.

"Sebastian, let me guide you, one last time" Yichén said, his voice stern as he handed me his amulet. "Listen to your instincts" he whispered as the amulet glowed blue, the familiar warmth was soothing and calming, the scent of fresh flowers and the taste of berries, Yichén and I was one again.

"This is what the gods wanted, Sebastian, the fight of good vs evil, you and Pazandir must face each other, one will die and one will live." Yichén's voice echoed in my mind, a fond reminder of our training

"No pressure" I replied, my sarcasm masking my nerves.

"Focus, use all your skills and all your strength"

Pazandir walked towards me and waited, the remainder of the soldiers from both sides gathered and parted leaving a wide circle. The ground was flat, perfect for combat.

I walked forward, handing my guns and blades to Cassandra. My breathing was fast and my palms were sweaty, the air was heavy and the wind was still, the heat was unbearable, a sticky humidity made the armour itch and cling to my body.

I took one last look at Cassandra, her face was worried, and the stress was evident.

"It's time" I took a deep breath and walked towards the middle of the circle, my boots crunching the dry dead earth, clumps of mud and rubble crumbling with each step.

We faced each other, no words were spoken, no weapons were drawn.

"You will die tonight, human." Pazandir snarled, his tone was low, and his voice was deep and raspy.

"Your reign ends here, monster," I replied before spitting the clammy ball of phlegm from my mouth.

"Your arrogance is astonishing, and your bravery is admirable, but I will enjoy watching life fade from your eyes."

"Bring it."

Pazandir coiled down and launched towards me, his arms out wide and his chest puffed out, his hands clapped together slamming the air trapped between them sending a gust that knocked me off my feet. I slammed onto my back and scrambled to stand. Pazandir charged, his fist connected to my face and sent me flying backwards, the pain was excruciating, my face felt like it had been torn open, his fist was rock solid, a force to be reckoned with.

"FIGHT BACK BOY!" Pazandir laughed.

He kicked the air and a wave of force smacked me in the chest, the impact cracked my rib, I could hear the snap as my bones were crushed, the pain sent a jolt coursing through my body. The sharp sensation rendered me motionless, I could only focus on the pain, a deep throb pulsated as my body recovered.

"I'm going to enjoy killing you"

My lungs burned and my breathing was shallow, the pain was immense, but I got back up.

"You will have to do better than that, Pazandir." I coughed up blood and wiped the crimson from my mouth.

Yichén's voice echoed.

"Don't forget your training, focus and use your senses"

"How do you defeat a being whose strength is greater than yours?" I asked.

"The fight is not always won by strength, Sebastian" Yichén replied, his words were true.

Pazandir walked forward, stomping loudly and rhythmically.

I took a deep breath and slowed my heart rate, it matched the pounding of his footsteps, a steady beat.

The smell of his sweat was salty and acidic, he was close.

I dodged his attack, a sweeping right, and kicked him in the shin, he laughed,

'Watch out! His sweeping leg, roll left and swing a right hook to his stomach and launch a roundhouse,' Yichén guided my attacks as I followed with precision.

Pazandir dropped to the ground, he coughed and wheezed, his breathing shallow. I reckon he wasn't accustomed to being beaten, never felt a blow from a formidable opponent.

"Not so big now, huh?"

He stood back up,

"Quickly, jab, hook and take his back. Hold a neck crank, tight as possible" I listened to the voice in my head and carried out the sequence, the sound of his joints popping and cracking as his neck was torqued, his screams filled the air, a satisfying sound.

Pazandir's men screamed and called for his release, the forces of Shíjiān and the army of shieldmaiden cheered as the fight continued in my favour.

Pazandir threw his back forward and flipped me off, the force winded me and the pain was immense, my grip was lost and I was flung to the ground, his neck was sore, but the job wasn't done.

"ENOUGH!" his knee rose high, above his head, his scream deafening, "AAARGH!" Pazandir drove his foot down with all his might and connected with my leg above the knee, severing the bone and ripping it clean off.

The pain was immeasurable, my leg was torn off and lay a metre away. The crowd gasped and screamed.

"SEBASTIAN! NO!" Cassandra cried.

The blood was gushing, I could see it pouring from the wound.

"Now you die" Pazandir spoke, his words were harsh, ruthless and calculated.

"I'm not finished yet," I said, as I rolled over, grabbing the blade hidden under my sleeve.

"What is this? Some cheap trick?" Pazandir said as I drove the blade into his shin and twisted, the wound opened and tore through his flesh, he cowered and screamed, I pulled back,

"Again, stab him again Sebastian" Yichén's voice was frantic and his words were rushed.

'Again' I listened and stabbed again, Pazandir cried, his agony was immense, the wounds were deep and messy, twisting the blade each time I tore tendons from bone.

"ENOUGH!" He lay on his back in a pool of his blood, choking and sputtering as words struggled to form and escape his mouth,

"You have won, spare me and I shall restore her, your love"

"What did you say?" His words startled me, his offer seemed acceptable, he darted his eyes behind me. Natasha stood there amongst the crowd, her beastly form towering and motionless, shackled in chains.

"Natasha!, I will restore her, bring her back to life." He gasped and rolled around in agony "Allow me to reside in hell, have mercy and you will be reunited"

"What about the prophecy?" I held his neck tight and forced him to the ground, stopping his pathetic writhing "Will I become all-powerful, Time and space?"

"No, only the chosen one can become the ruler, if you accept, you will have your former life, a life of peace"

I became overcome with emotion, the thought of having Natasha back, and living the life we had was too much to ignore. But the chance to rule and imbue myself with ultimate power was too sweet."

"Feel my blade, beast. May my wrath bring me power!" I slowly sunk my blade for one last time into Pazandir's throat, his life passing with each second as I pushed deeper.

"FOOL!" Pazandir flicked his wrist with his last motion, he squeezed the life from Natasha, her neck cranked in awkward motions, left to right, bones cracked and snapped, splintering into shards till her body fell limp.

I stood proud and overcome, wisps of power swirled around my blade, the power flowed through me, and the energy was exhilarating.

"Sebastian, what have you done!" Yichén's voice was full of hate and disappointment.

"What needs to be done?" I replied as the darkness consumed me. Scars cracked and ripped across my face, my eyes glowed white and my hair fell grey.

"I am the chosen one, the gods are fools." I laughed, as I looked upon the face of the defeated, the armies of Shíjiān bowed, the shieldmaidens knelt and the beast of shadow stood ready.

"My reign is eternal, my power is unmatched, and I will have my glory" I swung my blade through the air, with one fell swoop casting them all to darkness, their bodies turning to ash.

"And no one will stand in my way"

"You are no saviour, you are the monster, the prophecy spoke of," Yichén said, his face was blank and his heart was cold, "I want no part of this" he turned his back and walked away before I could attack, he disappeared.

With the power of time and space, I could change events, harness the outcome and manipulate the future. The power was incredible. My first task was ensuring my fate, I remembered my training, the moments that placed me to make the man I became. I slowed my heart rate and controlled my breathing, in and out, in and out. I remembered the place, the trees stood and towered in a perfect circle around a wooden pavilion, it stood in the middle, covered in vines and moss, held together by flora and fauna. I watched from afar as she nodded and stepped seductively into the structure, the sweet smell of Orange Blossom and Spanish Jasmine was intoxicating even from this distance. I remembered her lips, soft and arousing. Only then I understood why her body went limp as she begged for me to stop, I was a warning of events about to come. That's when I panicked, I made sure I saw myself in the distance before merging into the shadows, disappearing into the night, an immortal god left to roam the streets alone, like a dog, unwanted and unloved, my curse, my prize.

Scars

The wounds he bears, both seen and not,
Remind him of the battles fought.
The pain he feels, deep in his soul,
A heavy burden, taking its toll.

Yet still he rises, strong and true,
A hero through and through.
For though he bears the scars of war,
His spirit shines forever more.

Through the shadows he silently slinks,
A whispering ghost, he never blinks.
Time bends and contorts at his touch,
Leaving behind a feeling of clutch.

Printed in Dunstable, United Kingdom